DECISION

A St. Clair Thriller - Book 1

Ridge King

Series Reading Order
Available at
www.ridgeking.com

© *2020 Elsinore Press*
gppress@gmail.com

PRINCIPAL CHARACTERS

In the White House
Jeffrey Norwalk, Republican President of the U.S.
Eric Stathis, Chief of Staff
Phil Slanetti, Aide for Congressional Liaison

In the Republican Campaign
Sam Houston St. Clair, Governor of Florida, Republican
Candidate for President
Jack Houston St. Clair, his eldest son

In the Democratic Campaign
Frederick B. Thurston, Senator from Michigan,
Democratic candidate for President

In the Congress
Lamar LeGrand Perryman of Virginia, Speaker of the
House of Representatives
Matt Hawkins, Democratic Congressman of Wyoming

In the Diplomatic Corps
Lord Harold Ellsworth, British Ambassador
Fyodor Z. Kornilevski, Russian ambassador

Other Principal Characters
Patricia Vaughan, prominent socialite
Ramona Fuentes, prominent lawyer in Miami
Babylon Fuentes, her daughter, lover to Jack
Raven Fuentes, her older sister and Jack's former lover
Lieutenant Rafael St. Clair, Jack's younger brother, first
officer in USCGC *Fearless*
Derek Gilbertson, member of the Fuentes law firm,
former husband to Raven
Omer Flores, undercover DEA agent
Laurencio Duarte, undercover DEA agent

Article Two of the Constitution

"The Electors shall meet in their respective States, and vote by Ballot for two Persons, of whom one at least shall not be an Inhabitant of the same State with themselves. And they shall make a List of all the Persons voted for, and of the Number of Votes for each; which List they shall sign and certify, and transmit sealed to the Seat of the Government of the United States, directed to the President of the Senate.

"The President of the Senate shall, in the Presence of the Senate and House of Representatives, open all the Certificates, and the Votes shall then be counted.

"The Person having the greatest Number of Votes shall be the President, if such Number be a Majority of the whole Number of Electors appointed; and if no Person have a Majority, the said House of Representatives shall in like Manner choose the President. **But in choosing the President, the Votes shall be taken by <u>States</u>, with each State having one Vote."**

Table of Contents

PROLOGUE

"Matthew Hawkins, please, the White House calling."

Matt felt a growl come from his stomach. He knew it was a hunger pang, but he felt a sudden nausea come over him.

"Uh..."

"Is this Mr. Hawkins?"

"Yes... Is this some kind of prank?"

"No, sir."

"Well, who the hell wants to talk to me from the White House?"

He shot a suspicious look at Jack Houston St. Clair, who shook his head and held out his hands and shrugged as if he didn't know *anything* about this.

"The President," came the measured response from a White House operator who had heard the same reaction before.

Matt's mind went numb at the sound of the words: THE PRESIDENT.

His eyes glazed over and he stared straight ahead, almost unaware what was happening, what he was hearing.

"*The President?*" he mumbled.

"Yes, sir. Please hold while I connect you."

Matt stood still, looking down at the phone on the table below him, frowning, suddenly overcome with a case of nervousness mixed with his hunger. His head floated with the feeling, like a smoker's first cigarette in the morning.

"Matt Hawkins?"

"Yes, uh, yes, this is he," he replied, suddenly coming to. He knew that husky voice.

"This is President Norwalk, Matt. I'm sorry to ask you on such short notice, but would it be possible for you to come see me?"

"See you, sir, I mean, Mr. President?"

"Yes."

"Uh, when should I come?"

"As soon as you can. Right now if you can."

"Right now?"

"Yes, Matt," said Norwalk a little impatiently. *"If you can."*

"Oh, yes, sir, I can come now."

"I'm not interrupting you, am I?" asked Norwalk.

"No, Mr. President, I'm just here with Jack Houston St. Clair. He's been trying to—"

"Trying to get you to vote for his dad, right?"

"Yes, Mr. President."

"Well, tell him I've got his dad sitting outside my office. Why don't you just bring Jack along with you?"

"All right, Mr. President, I will."

"Good, I'll expect you in fifteen minutes."

Matt's mind was in a whirl.

"At the White House, Mr. President?"

"Yes, Matt, at the White House. That's where I have my office," said Norwalk indulgently, quickly adding: "I can send a car."

"No, sir. We'll just take a taxi."

"Very good."

He rang off.

Matt replaced the receiver with a clatter, finding the cradle after a few seconds, feeling for it but not really seeing it.

"And you're saying you don't know anything about this, Jack?"

"Swear to God," said Jack.

"He says your dad is sitting right outside the Oval Office."

"I don't know anything about that, either," said Jack.

Matt gave him a skeptical look.

"He wants me to bring you over with me."

"Fine. But did he say what he wanted?"

"Don't you think that's pretty obvious?"

"Yeah, he's gonna lean on you somehow, I guess."

"Should I go?"

"You told him you were coming."

"Yeah."

"And you're gonna have to face the music eventually."

"Yeah, I guess."

"Then let's go see what the old man has on his scheming little mind," said Jack.

Matt turned and walked towards the door and put his hand on the knob to turn it. He opened it and stood in the doorway thinking: *What could he possibly have to say to me?* He was nervous, fearful, unsure, hesitant. Matt couldn't believe, couldn't comprehend that he was attracting so much attention for his one lousy vote. It simply didn't register that *he* could be so important that the President himself would have to intervene. He was saturated with apprehension, fear and elation.

He glided to the elevator in a daze, following Jack, reached the lobby and walked outside mechanically to take a taxi. The cold air and bright sunshine outside hit him forcibly and he realized he hadn't even put on his topcoat. He stepped into the taxi after Jack.

"Where to, bud?" asked the driver looking at him through his rearview mirror.

Matt sat in the back seat looking straight ahead. "What?"

"Where to?"

"Oh yes, the White House."

He glanced at Jack, who wore a thin smile.

Matt half thought that a magic carpet would pick him up and deposit him on the White House lawn. He didn't notice the impressed driver's eyebrows rise as he drove off and joined the traffic on Connecticut Avenue for the short drive to the White House.

"Well, this is a first," said the cabbie.

"What?" asked Matt.

"Twenty-six years driving a cab in D.C. and nobody *ever*—not *once*—gets in my cab and says, 'Take me to the White House.' Not one single time."

"No?"

"No. I tellya, it's a first for me."

9

"That makes three of us," said Jack with a crooked smile.

What could he say to Norwalk when he asked him to switch his vote? Could he just say "No" to him?

Matt rolled down the window to let the freezing air in. He breathed deeply, trying to restore his senses, which remained dulled to the point of numbness all over. He decided he would just tell the President that he'd made up his mind and that he would appreciate it if the White House would let him vote his way without any interference.

He felt his weakness and hated it. He gently massaged his forehead and then pounded his head with his fist. Everything was so sudden. He should've put off Norwalk a day or two. But no one put off the President when he called. *You had to be ready,* thought Matt. *You had to be ready when they threw you a curve. If you couldn't measure up, you were out. They walked all over you and you were out, out, out!*

"*Hey, mister!*" said the cabbie for the second time.

"Huh, what?"

He focused on the cabbie, who looked over the seat at him and jerked his head backwards towards his window. Matt looked out. A uniformed guard was looking in at him through the cabbie's window.

"Your name, sir?"

"I have an appointment with the President," said Matt.

"Yes, sir, *but what is your name?*" asked the guard, who recognized that Hawkins had never been to the White House before.

"Oh, Matthew Hawkins."

The guard looked at Jack.

"And Jack Houston St. Clair."

"Thank you, sir." He consulted his clipboard. "If you'll leave the cab, we'll take you up from here."

Matt paid the fare and got out. The cab made a U-turn and left the grounds. An enclosed golf cart pulled up and Matt got in after Jack.

Matt's attention was fixed on the curving driveway ahead as the golf cart moved along it. The White House stood out massive and solid before him, the top of it seemed lost to his peripheral vision as they got closer. The cart stopped and the doors snapped open as if by magic. He fumbled his way out and followed one of the guards who led them toward the Mansion.

They gave their names and another guard made a telephone call as they were led to a waiting room in the old part of the White House. They sat alone in a room furnished with fine antiques and carpeted with one large Persian rug.

Matt wondered why they were alone. Surely there must be others waiting to see the President.

In a moment a man entered. They stood.

"How do you do, Mr. Hawkins? And Mr. St. Clair?"

They all shook hands.

"I'm Charles Roebuck, the President's appointments secretary."

Matt nodded and said, "Hello." Jack just nodded.

Matt recognized Roebuck's face now. He remembered seeing his picture in the papers.

"Please follow me, gentlemen," said Roebuck, moving away gracefully. They walked alongside him down a long, richly furnished corridor to the West Wing.

"The President forgot to tell you which gate to use, Mr. Hawkins. You came in the formal entrance. I had to run down here to get you," Roebuck said affably.

"Oh, I'm sorry."

"Oh no, it's nothing. He seldom meets with people who haven't been here before. It never crops up," said the secretary with a friendly smile. He didn't recognize how much Hawkins felt his remark. Matt felt the unique nature of his visit. *He was a nobody.* On the same level as the Boy Scouts coming to get an award from the President. They have to be told which gate to use.

They entered the West Wing and Matt noticed how much more like a normal business office the surroundings looked, only the ceilings were high and imposing. Expensive moldings. People were coming and going until they reached the area around the Oval Office itself, which was quieter.

"I'll take you right into the Oval Office, Mr. Hawkins. The President's been expecting you," said Roebuck, approaching a thoroughly unprepossessing white door. "Mr. St. Clair, you can join your father. He's waiting in the anteroom just through that door."

"Thank you," said Jack.

"Wish me luck," Matt smiled.

Jack took a long look at the naïve Wyomingite.

"Gook luck, Matt."

Roebuck turned and opened the thick door into the Oval Office.

As Jack turned to go where he was told, he caught a glimpse of President Norwalk sitting behind his desk. A thought raced through his mind:

He's going to eat that boy alive.

SIX WEEKS EARLIER

Chapter 1
General Yin

General Yin concluded his conversation and put the telephone down. He called the staff in. The general rose and walked around the desk. He turned and spoke with authority, but quietly, earnestly.

"I have been ordered to proceed with the operation just as it has been outlined to you. Although you are all aware that the international situation is extremely volatile, we must prepare ourselves and our units to move fast when called upon.

"You will understand, then, the highest importance our superiors are placing on political negotiations. It is with this background in mind that I again urge you all to the efficient performance of your duties. By efficient I mean quiet. Move over to the map one more time, all of you."

Yin looked at their faces, staring down at the map. How young they were. How ignorant they were. What did they know of the blood the desert had soaked up in the old days?

The staff marveled at General Yin's maps. Every detail was noted, every piece of artillery, every supply route. In colors alternate supply routes were marked, as well as secret depots with supplies buried in the

Xinjiang desert. Many of the marks existed only on his maps.

"Comrades," the general continued when they were all in place, "you will note the proximity of our future positions to the Kazakhstan border. You are all closely acquainted with the underground network along and near the border between our tunnels at Huocheng and the Russian buildup across the border at Zharkent. You must have all your units established underground by morning and out of sight of Russian air reconnaissance. The Russians know about the network of tunnels, but they are not sure of their location, length, size or capacity. Since the Russians have begun to build up the Kazakh border positions, Beijing wants us to be in position if they cross. While in the tunnels, we will remain on full alert. I believe you understand why we are moving now."

The general straightened himself and turned slightly to sit on the table.

"All attention is focused on America. This has eased our position here in the Xinjiang somewhat, but as Moscow and Beijing look to Washington, we cannot expect the same thing from our counterparts across the border. Let me discuss with you the importance of this most recent concentration of Russian troops in Kazakhstan."

With this he looked back at his maps and bent over the table.

"If the Russians move the bulk of their troops along the border, say, above Mongolia or above Manchuria, we may be able to move out of Xinjiang very soon and leave the Regional Militia to defend the area. I have always doubted the Russian High

Command would ever do this because in the north, what is it they are protecting from Chinese invasion? They are protecting the Great Siberian *Plateau*, which they neither wish to defend, nor we to attack. Across Kazakhstan, however, lies the most direct route to Moscow, through the Kazakh Hills. To the north of the Kazakh Hills lies the Great Siberian *Plain*, the heart of Russian agriculture. The Russian base, then, will remain here," he stabbed a point on the map, "in the regional capital of Almaty. Since we have news of the Russian advance to the border town of Zharkent, we will go to our tunnels and await their movements. When they withdraw, we will withdraw."

The general sighed, weary with the constant game of hide-and-seek he and the Russian armies played along their mutual border which, when it was the Soviet Union, stretched across the face of Asia from Afghanistan to the Koreas. It had gotten much worse since the break-up of the Soviet Union. At least then there had been one army—now there was the Russian Army as well as the independent republics' armies, but Yin knew it was worse for the Russians coordinating maneuvers and looking out for ruffled feathers than it was for him.

General Yin remained for several minutes leaning over his map table, his eyes squinting down as he surveyed the terrain of the Kazakh Hills, the marshy area around the mouth of the Ili River and Lake Balkhash. Suddenly he spoke to his staff again, as if having forgotten they were there.

"Report to your units."

Placing his pencil on the map, he stood straight again. His staff came to full attention around him. He jerked his chin slightly upwards in what looked like a nervous twitch, but his staff immediately recognized they had been dismissed. They were all particularly happy to have the heavy-handed expertise of General Yin on this silent desert campaign. By staying out of politics, Yin had remained alive and in power long enough to be considered the greatest tactician in the Red Army.

The door closed behind the last of his staff, leaving the general alone. He walked over to the window behind his desk and looked out. He was a short man with fine, gray hair. He had to stand on his toes to unlock the window. Lifting it, he put his elbows on the windowsill and looked west out across the desert into the eye of the sinking sun. His military enclave was on the western outskirts of Ürümqi and his office was in a small wooden building. He saw nothing but the desert stretching out to the west. A couple of hundred miles in that direction was the Kazakhstan frontier, and beyond that the high road to Moscow, a road he had never seen except on a thousand maps all his life and a road he hoped he would never see.

A wind was getting up and the sand whipped the few brush plants that hardly obscured the general's vision as he looked into the slowly fading light of the desert. The general, so old now after many bitter and difficult campaigns, found himself reflecting that with the full moon expected tonight, the desert would be a beautiful place through which to travel. The desert would not be as safe with a full moon, but he didn't worry about that because he couldn't do anything about it. From his window, the desert was lovely in the twilight. It had not always been so lovely. Its serenity cloaked a bloody past. Yin's own father, a decorated general himself, told him stories of the slaughter in the desert, of Mao's command to drive hundreds of thousands of fleeing peasants into the desert where they preferred to die of thirst rather than return to be butchered.

So many struggles.

General Yin knew that the Russians had upwards of three million troops and that about a million of them hovered on China's border.

Against that one million Russians, Yin had two and a half million troops ready to field with an easy three million to match the Russian reserve. But even with such a vast superiority in manpower, Yin knew he would lose a long war with the enemy. The superior Russian armor, artillery and other matériel would overwhelm the vast Chinese hosts.

He had been in the Xinjiang now for two months with occasional trips northeast to Chining where several hundred thousand men were deployed ready to march into "independent" Mongolia to stop any Russian advance from the north. In the Xinjiang his forces were made up of many old tribes and former blood enemies crushed into obedience by the current regime: Uyghurs, Kazakhs (the same tribe that largely peopled Kazakhstan), the Tajik, Huis, Mongols and Uzbeks. He had trained them well and knew they would fight hard and, if necessary, to the last man. But it hurt him to think of them going by the hundreds of thousands against strafing fire from Russian fighters because his own outnumbered air forces would be driven from the skies. There were fourteen million people in the Xinjiang Uyghur Autonomous Region; it was General Yin Feng-hsu's job to make sure they remained "autonomous."

The sun sank majestically over the horizon. There was a knock.

"Enter."

A colonel entered with a piece of paper.

"The final weather report, Comrade General."

"Yes," said Yin, not raising his head, which he cupped in the palms of his hands as he leaned on the windowsill.

"Sunset," reported the colonel, "will be in three and one-half minutes, there will be no rain, clear skies, but wind up to fifteen mile per hour gusts. And a full moon."

"No rain. And yet this entire operation, the coming war itself is all about water. Water, water, water—and here we are in the middle of the desert to fight for water."

The general laughed. The colonel laughed with him, having no idea what the general was laughing about.

"Yes," said the general, looking out into the desert. He turned quickly and suddenly from the window. This sudden movement surprised the colonel, but General Yin didn't notice the colonel's surprise, for his mind was elsewhere. On an afterthought, the general turned around, lowered the window and stood on his toes and locked it. He turned back to his desk and began to collect his papers.

"Ten minutes after the official sunset time, Comrade Colonel, you will issue orders to all units to move out."

"Yes, Comrade General."

"As soon as you have done that, return here with the staff and help me with my papers and maps. We must move rapidly to be in place by morning, Colonel."

General Yin turned for a final look at the sinking sun.

"It is time."

Chapter 2
General Tulevgin

About three hundred fifty miles northwest of General Yin, Field Marshal Vladimir Tulevgin was riding south towards the Xinjiang border. Under the field marshal's direct command were one and a half million of Russia's three million troops. They were scattered along the 1,400 mile long border that the former Soviet Union (and now the independent republics) shared with China. He had well over half a million troops at his immediate disposal in Kazakhstan alone.

Surprising the officers of his senior staff, Field Marshal Tulevgin abruptly ordered the driver to pull over to the side of the road out of the way of the troop transports, tanks and trucks which continued to move south. Several cars containing the rest of the staff pulled over in turn.

The officers poured out of the big JDV-80 cars and watched with intense interest as their leader ordered a portable table set up and his maps laid out. They watched as this hulk of a man removed his hat and put it, together with his baton, on the table beside the maps. He had a head of gloriously furry hair, which made his already overbearing six-feet-four-inch height seem staggering. The sixty-five year old field marshal, an oft-decorated hero, stood hunched over the table with both hands, palms down, on the maps. His greatcoat fell heavy and massive from his high shoulders to the ground.

Any wandering minds were quickly brought back to the present moment as Tulevgin slowly straightened himself. As he stood, he revealed a twisted frown on his face that scarcely concealed the fury inside him.

Tulevgin had many things on his mind. He was angry, threatened, uninformed, frustrated, beset with tedium – but also excited. He was angry because he'd been forced to meet with elected officials in Almaty that morning, and with others in the national capital of Astana the morning before. He'd been ordered by Moscow to keep the local officials informed on his movements.

What could officials in Almaty or Astana do for him except waste his time and get in his way?

But he agreed to the meeting so he wouldn't ruffle any feathers in Moscow. The local officials didn't know what to ask and since Field Marshal Tulevgin offered nothing to them in the way of information about troop movements or activities or plans, he and his staff simply ate breakfast with the local government and promptly filed out of the hall, into their JDV-80 military cars, and away to the airport where Tulevgin flew far north to inspect some installations before driving south by car and ordering the advance to Zharkent.

Tulevgin was threatened because recent messages from Moscow seemed to shift much of the burden for the solution of the entire Chinese problem to his shoulders. He was in a quandary. He couldn't move forward beyond Zharkent and he couldn't move back. There was of course no need to move back because the Chinese were not moving forward and weren't about to do so, thought Tulevgin, so long as their crazed superiors in Beijing kept their heads about them. He was well aware at this stage political negotiations mattered much more than military movements. And yet, he was extremely uneasy about his position because he had ambitions, political ambitions, far beyond his present status in the military, which already conferred upon him enough political power to acquire the envy of many shrewd and devious men. Tulevgin firmly decided to return to Moscow as soon as the American position became a little clearer.

The field marshal felt uninformed and desperately lacking any new information from his intelligence unit. Moscow had ordered an all but complete cessation of air reconnaissance flights over Chinese territory until the Kremlin could be surer about the American position. The Kremlin didn't want to take the blame for any accidents that might happen because the already aggravated international situation could not be strained any further. Tulevgin was limited to a handful of air reconnaissance missions per day along the entire fourteen hundred mile border. This crippled him.

He was aware that General Yin was in Ürümqi, or on the outskirts of it somewhere in a desert tunnel, but he only felt sure of this because he kept his own whereabouts quite publicized. With the Russian military advantage, he felt sure that Yin would be following him wherever he trekked, up and down the long, long border, fearing that trouble could not be far from Tulevgin's headquarters. He was aware of the tunnel network near Huocheng, but he lacked much information on that network. It was built in the 1950s when China and Russia enjoyed better relations, and the Russians at that time didn't quite see how they could investigate without making the whole inquiry look a little bit unseemly.

Looking at the long-range situation, however, Tulevgin was more frustrated about the strategy worked out some years ago in the Kremlin. The bulk of Russian military strength was centered in the northern part of the Kazakh Republic so that quick swings could be made to reinforce other units defending the Kazakh Hills to the south and the Great Siberian Plain to the direct north, both of which areas the Kremlin considered vital for the country to survive a prolonged attack. This, true as it was, still placed the Russian Army in an unenviable position of having to counterattack into the heart of the Xinjiang, one of the great arid wastes of Asia. As a long-term danger, this annoyed the field marshal.

On top of this the man was just plain bored with running up and down the long border day after day, week after week, month after month. Yes, he thought to himself, as soon as the Kremlin knows more about the American position, he would get firm orders to move.

He stopped pacing and faced his staff, addressing them with superfluous stiffness.

"We will continue towards Zharkent near the Xinjiang frontier and we will proceed to establish our headquarters there." Two colonels looked at each other and shrugged. Then Tulevgin walked back to his map, looked at it briefly, grunted, took up his hat and placed it on his head, scooped up his baton and struck the table twice with it. While the field marshal returned to his car, two officers collected the maps as another folded the table. In a moment all the cars were back in the column of onrushing vehicles, but this time their lights were on, for dusk had fallen while the field marshal paced. In his car, Tulevgin asked his chief of staff what time he thought they would get to Zharkent. The COS said in about an hour and a half. Tulevgin thought that was excellent, because he wanted to get plenty of sleep that night so he could inspect the Chinese border personally the next morning.

Chapter 3
In the Capitals

Meanwhile, the forbidding walls of the Kremlin were topped with snow. Inside, the President met in secret session with his closest advisors to discuss the current deterioration of relations between Moscow and Beijing. Also on the agenda was the position of the American government. Nothing was decided. The conversation throughout centered on monumental "ifs." It was determined that the group would meet again the next morning in secret session to discuss the outcome of the American election.

Back in his office, the President sent a top secret scrambled cable to the Russian ambassador to the United States, Fyodor Z. Kornilevski. It read in part, "You will notify us, as previously requested, of any and all significant developments tonight and tomorrow morning. Owing to the extreme delicacy of the international situation at the present time, we require that you do anything you are able to do— including extreme measures—to forward our position in this matter." Then the President, after a brief meeting with his foreign minister, went home to bed.

The winter sun had set in Moscow.

* * *

In Cairo that afternoon an important CIA agent met one of his operatives in a little-known coffee bar off Marigalzu Avenue. Information was received and orders given as the senior agent mopped the perspiration off his forehead with a white handkerchief. Then they talked just like two ordinary persons who might be interested in the latest political developments in Egypt.

In the Middle East at this moment there were some interesting political decisions being formulated. On this day there had been a summit meeting of the Arab League to discuss how they would react to events occurring in Russia, the United States and China. What this meant to everyone in the world was the ultimate destination of the vast Middle Eastern oil reserves necessary to everyone in the world, and certainly vital to any nation that hoped to remain dominant.

* * *

In Paris, the President of France met briefly with his minister for foreign affairs in the Elysée Palace. Back in the ministry building, the minister dictated a dispatch to his ambassador in Washington. When he left his office it was night and he was already late for a reception at the Polish Embassy.

* * *

In London, the foreign minister had just concluded the dictation of a similar note to his government's representative in Washington before heading out to meet his wife for a concert (another dull Mahler symphony) at Royal Albert Hall.

Chapter 4
Deadlock!

In all centers of political and military power, every practiced eye was directed to the United States on this night. These eyes always regarded the United States with close attention, but every fourth November that attention turned into zealous scrutiny. For all day long in the United States was General Election Day. No one at home or abroad had been able to make any decisions all day. Individuals waited, emperors, princes, kings and Presidents and their ministers of state the world around watched silently, their policies in abeyance; armies stood quietly; governments paused to observe while America voted.

The excitement and tension in an American election came not during the polling, as it does in unstable countries, but in the tabulation of the votes. The artificial drama that came from merely counting votes seemed to grow more intense with each passing election.

By 2 A.M., there was no declared winner. Almost everyone in the United States not yet asleep watched TV. People who didn't ordinarily watch TV had put down their books or esoteric magazines to sit goofy-eyed inches from their sets. Even honeymooning couples found something more important than themselves—on TV. No one in America had ever lived through what was happening.

The bleary-eyed anchor on NBC News, Aaron Cross, was speaking, listening into his earpiece at the same time.

"I've just been informed that the latest analysis has predicted the outcome of the Presidential race in Oklahoma, New Jersey and California, the last states to come in," he said. The camera cut to each state's figures on the tabulation board. Checkmarks appeared suddenly by a candidate's name. The camera then cut to the master board that showed cumulative popular voting and Electoral College tallies. The anchor's voice spoke over the picture before the camera cut back to him.

"According to our figures, and I don't believe what I'm saying, *there appears to be a tie for President!*" As he said those words, he imagined a great breathless hush spreading across the land. "We are having all our computer predictions checked to be sure we haven't made a mistake." His voice was rushed and excited. "*The Electoral College is deadlocked!*" he said emotionally. "*There is no winner!*"

He called on Chuck Todd, the NBC News political director, to help him explain to the American people the peculiar legal technicality that could produce such an unheralded, unexpected and exasperating deadlocked election. (Producers in the control booth hurriedly scanned their list of experts to find people with knowledge about this esoteric conundrum.)

Chuck Todd, meanwhile, sat somber-faced before the cameras and explained that without a majority in the Electoral College, neither candidate could win the election. Of course, one candidate was ahead of the other in the *popular* vote, but under the American system, that didn't matter.

Most of their listeners had heard of the Electoral College at one time or another, but most didn't know what role it played.

"According to the Constitution," was a phrase Americans heard over and over all night. The experts explained that the Constitution directed the House of Representatives to vote to determine who would be President. Each state would have only one vote, so small states suddenly became very powerful. Excited reporters and commentators were discussing all the ramifications on television. Congress was not to meet until January. Who would be the President-elect? How would the quiet transfer of power that normally characterized an American election be carried out? No one knew.

Chapter 5
Senator Thurston

The senior senator from Michigan, Frederick B. Thurston, stared into a black cup of coffee. He watched reflected light flicker across the surface of the black liquid and disappear. He had come too far, too soon to lose an election this close without a fight, and he meant to use every back alley trick he'd ever learned from his blue-collar childhood to the rarefied air of the Senate to win.

He considered himself lucky to be the Democratic nominee. That honor rarely fell onto the shoulders of a forty-one year old up-and-comer. He knew most of the tricks already because he was a quick study and because in Michigan politics he had to learn faster than someone from Utah.

High up in the Pacific Arms Hotel in the dirty city of Detroit, Fredrick Thurston looked up from his coffee cup. His six-foot, one-inch body was lean and lithe. His skin did not yet sag anywhere on his body, except perhaps a little under the eyes, but that could be attributed to the frenetic pace of the last few days of the campaign. So could the condition of his muscles, which pulled and ached under his skin. His right forearm and hand were red and callused, having been shaken, yanked, pulled, scratched (and bitten twice) during the campaign. His neatly trimmed hair, wavy and black, hadn't been combed in five hours.

For the past hour, he'd been secluded in a sitting room in the hotel with his closest staff members examining the election returns. There was Jesse Epstein, his campaign manager, who went back ten years with Thurston as his original administrative assistant when he was a freshman congressman; Terry McAvoy, his press secretary, with his perfectly straight, well-cut red hair; Brian Gilbert, his long-time law partner in Detroit, personal friend and advisor; and Steven Ressler, a toy manufacturer from New York who was introduced to him by McAvoy three years ago. Ressler helped with Thurston's campaign for reelection to the Senate two years earlier and was now a top strategist.

"What time is it?" Thurston asked no one in particular.

"Three o'clock," McAvoy answered.

"Well, let's take it from the top," Thurston said after a pause.

Epstein shuffled dozens of papers in his hands and raised his head with a skeptical look that always characterized him. He was a short, dark-haired man with pudgy cheeks and full lips.

"Are you going down to the ballroom?" asked McAvoy, the press aide. "They've been screaming at me all night."

"No, not yet," said Thurston. "Let's have a rundown, Jess."

"Right," said Epstein, looking down at his papers and figures. "We'll win the popular vote."

"Who gives a fuck … now?" asked Thurston wearily.

"Right, that doesn't make any difference now. We've taken twenty-six states to St. Clair's twenty-four, and that won't make any difference, either. With the electoral vote even, the only way to keep it out of the House is for one or more electors to go against somebody. That shouldn't happen because of all the state laws around to make them keep their word, but if we could get only one to come over to us in a state that doesn't have such a law, we could keep it out of the House."

"St. Clair's people will try whatever we try," said Gilbert.

"We'll know by morning or tomorrow afternoon if we can count on all our people, and who on the other side might be," Ressler used the word archly, "*persuaded* to join us."

"If the electors start breaking ranks, it'll end up in court," said Epstein.

"We don't want to see Bush-Gore again," said McAvoy.

Thurston put his cup down on a side table and fell into a chair opposite Epstein, who spread all his papers out on top of other papers, reports and files on the coffee table.

"If it's that much in doubt, I think we better support straight voting in the Electoral College and take our chances in the House. We ought to do better there, anyway. We have a great majority in the House, and I'd rather have a big majority there than one vote in the College. I'm just worried to death over some little elector somewhere who thinks he can play king-maker."

Epstein looked hard at Thurston.

"What's the matter, Jess?"

"I just want everybody to remember one thing. This election year, *everybody's* going to be a kingmaker, whether it's decided in a recount, in the College or in the House. Just don't anybody hurt anybody else's little ego. We're gonna need them all."

"You're right, Jess. Let's go on."

"Well, let's take it from New England and work our way across," Epstein began. There were knocks at the door. McAvoy jumped up and answered it, admitting not only the pretty head of Peggy Thurston, but also the sounds of dozens of voices, telephones ringing and computer printers from the room beyond.

"Can I come in?" she asked, peeking round the door.

Thurston got up and crossed the room and kissed her.

"Not now, dear," he said. "We're trying to work out a little strategy. I was going to call you and tell you to get some sleep. Why don't you?"

"I thought I'd wait up. You'll have to go downstairs, won't you?"

"Yes, but not for an hour or so."

"I'll wait up for you, then we'll both go to sleep."

"Okay, honey, we'll be out in a little while." He kissed her again.

She left and McAvoy closed the door. Thurston went back to his chair and sat down again, rolling up his shirtsleeves. McAvoy resumed his lethargic position on the sofa.

"Okay," said Thurston, trying to relax by leaning back. There was another knock at the door. "God damn it!" he said, sitting up. He motioned to Steve Ressler with his head. "Get out there, will you, Steve? And tell them to leave me alone in here until I get ready. No exceptions." Ressler jumped up and went to the door, opened it, and pushed the man there out as he talked to him, closing the door behind him as he went.

"All right, let's try again."

"Breaking the nation up into the usual eight regions, it lines up like this. In the Northeast, six states. Out of those, we took only Massachusetts. They got Maine, Connecticut, New Hampshire, Vermont and Rhode Island. It was close in Rhode Island, but it's theirs. Out of five Middle Atlantic States, they got only Pennsylvania. We took the rest: New York, New Jersey, Maryland, Delaware. Thank God for little states like Delaware or we wouldn't have a tie. In the South's ten states, we took most: Arkansas, Florida, Mississippi, the Carolinas, Texas and Virginia. They took Alabama, Georgia and Louisiana. The real clincher down there is Louisiana. It's never voted Republican – ever! There's one Republican representative. Everybody else is a Democrat: two senators, the governor, all the other congressmen. Nobody voted along traditional lines. It's this damned foreign shit!"

Thurston lit a cigarette.

"I didn't believe it about Louisiana, either," he said. "Difference in votes?"

"Fifty, sixty thousand."

"Not enough to contest."

"No, that's a lot down there."

"Go on."

"In the five Border States, they took Oklahoma, no surprise. We got Kentucky, Missouri, Tennessee, West Virginia."

"Did all right there," McAvoy commented. Steve Ressler opened the door and returned, sitting in a corner behind a writing table. Epstein continued.

"In the Midwest, we got it bad. They got Illinois, Ohio, Wisconsin and Indiana. We kept Michigan and Minnesota. Six states there. The Farm States: Iowa, Nebraska, the Dakotas. We lost them all." Epstein paused and shook his head sadly. "I'd have bet my mother's teeth we had Iowa and North Dakota, especially in this election. Our polls showed they hated the Russians four to one out there. You know how those people feel."

"You never really know how they feel until they vote," said Thurston, quietly and with no trace of emotion. He crunched the butt of his cigarette in a tray. "You forgot Kansas."

"Yeah, sorry: we lost Kansas, too. The eight Mountain States. They took Colorado, Utah, Wyoming. We took the rest: Montana, Idaho, Nevada, Arizona and New Mexico."

"Surprise, surprise," said Thurston quietly, referring to what they all knew without having to say it. They expected to take both Colorado and Utah easily.

"Then the last five states out West."

Ressler lowered his eyes as if feeling pain, for he and the others all knew what Epstein was going to say.

"We got Hawaii and Alaska. They got the rest." He half-crumpled the papers in a helpless gesture and leaned his aching back slowly against the rear of the sofa. They'd lost California, Oregon and Washington. Each state hurt a lot, and all had been undecided that morning.

The rundown revealed in a more formal and cohesive way what had come to them separately and in bits and pieces all night long, from the very first few returns in Maine and New Hampshire. People were indecisive, angry, confused over the foreign issue and seemed to have voted on the basis of that alone. All predictions based on past data were now proved useless in helping to foresee the crazy way in which the states had combined to bring about the present haphazard situation.

Thurston stood up, put his hands in his back trouser pockets and began pacing back and forth. His tie long since had been jerked loose. He sweated in the warm room.

"Gut feeling – we're going to the House."

"I've already got people going over our files on all congressmen, both sides of the aisle," said Epstein.

"Good," remarked Thurston, still pacing. "We'll be doing a lot of face time with them between now and the new session. How much material on the freshmen coming up?"

"Plenty," said Gilbert, "but we'll get more."

"Get a *lot* more," smiled Thurston. "After a week or so we'll know the exact final vote, and if it's with us, we'll lay it on thick, raise some hell!" Thurston's voice began to move faster, rising a little in pitch. The aides knew he was ready to give orders.

"We'll have to come out supporting changes in the Constitution to get rid of the Electoral College, moving for direct popular vote. The small states will kill it, but we have to say it."

"You've been against that in the past," noted McAvoy.

"I just changed my mind. Once the popular vote is in and pretty definite, we'll move for recounts where we think we have much better than even chances. Less than that and we won't move."

"Right," said Ressler, who would have his staff begin arranging details the next day.

"For now we plan as if we're going to the House. Terry, go out and announce that I'll be coming downstairs shortly."

Terry McAvoy jumped up, found his coat somewhere in a corner on the floor, and straightened his tie before leaving the room in a rush.

"After I talk downstairs -- oh, something on the order of carrying this thing right through to the end, fighting for principles, all that crap -- Brian, you get Niles Overton and Stan Rifkin on the phone. Thank God they were reelected."

Niles Overton of Minnesota was majority leader of the House. Stan Rifkin of New Mexico was majority whip.

"I'll have to talk to them tonight. After them, I'll talk to Lamar Perryman."

"What's Perryman got to do with any of it?" asked Epstein. He never liked the inimitable, irascible congressman from Virginia.

Thurston stopped pacing and looked at Epstein.

"Because I've decided he's going to be speaker in the new Congress."

The room erupted in protest.

When the noise subsided, Ressler spoke.

"Fred, you can't be sure of Perryman. Nobody can. Why him and not Niles? It's supposed to be Niles since the old man died. Everybody knows that. *Shit, Perryman didn't even endorse you!"*

Ressler referred to the "old man," who was the former speaker of the House. This venerable congressman died during the campaign before Congress adjourned. Overton was majority leader at the time and Perryman merely a congressman with a powerful committee chairmanship. When the speaker was struck, less than two weeks before adjournment, Perryman was elevated to the chair at the old speaker's personal request for the remainder of the session. The honor was designed to cap Perryman's long career.

Thurston's suggestion to keep Perryman in the chair shocked everyone because the man was known to be fiercely independent. He bowed to no one, had a mind of his own, and his position on the Sino-Russian situation was even at this late date unclear.

"I am aware that he didn't endorse me, but he hasn't endorsed anyone for years, and he certainly isn't for St. Clair. The main point is to keep Overton free prior to the session so he can work on individuals. If Overton tells the caucus to go with

Perryman, it will. After the election, Perryman will resign and Overton will take the chair the way it was supposed to be. Brian, after I talk to Perryman, have White ready."

"Got it."

It would be unseemly for him not to call his running mate, the Honorable Dexter White, Governor of Nebraska, so he would do it, in its proper turn of importance.

Last.

"And that ought to do it," he said. Gilbert and Ressler were scribbling notes. Epstein found a cigarette somewhere inside his messy clothes and started smoking it after bumming a light from Gilbert. Thurston went into the bathroom nearby and washed his hands and face a long time until soap obliterated his features. He dried himself, combed his hair and arranged his clothing, getting his coat from the closet.

"You ready?" asked Epstein. Thurston nodded. Epstein went over and opened the door. Gilbert and Ressler went out.

"Jess," said Thurston as Epstein was leaving, "will you ask Peggy to come in here? Then we'll go down."

"Sure," said Epstein as he closed the door behind him. Peggy Thurston came in half a minute later, fresh, beautiful, blonde, creamy-skinned, and bringing with her the scent of fine perfume. Really upper crust, thought Thurston to himself as he looked at her coming to him. He wondered how she always managed to smell so fresh after these long election nights, and especially this one.

They hugged each other and kissed deeply.

"How *are* you?" she asked, with a mildly worried look coming into her eyes.

He laughed from his throat, deeply, quietly.

"I haven't been asked that all night. Every time it's been, 'How's it goin'?'"

"Well, I'm asking you. How are you? How do you feel about it?"

He broke away from her softly, rubbing his upper lip with a forefinger, and walked over to look out the window at the dingy cityscape. Most of the lights in the buildings downtown had been off for hours. A few blocks away he could see into the only lighted floor of a tall office building. A cleaning woman in a long, shabby dress and a scarf around her hair was dusting a desk. More than likely, he thought, that woman did not even vote today, had no interest whatsoever in who was elected President of the United States or which party might control the new Congress, or cared even slightly what the FTC, FAA, CIA or ICC might do tomorrow to change her life and the lives of millions of others. If she was even legally in the country.

"I really don't know how to feel," he said, holding his forehead with his left hand. "I know what I'm going to say downstairs in the ballroom," he chuckled, darkly, sardonically. "I always know what I'm going to say in public, don't I? But I don't know how I feel. It's so unexpected, this, this tie."

He drew his lips tightly over his gums as he clenched a fist. Several times without stopping he hit the back of the heavily padded armchair where he'd been sitting.

"This damned feeling of having it *so close* and yet still being able to lose it is what gets to me." He looked at her almost pleadingly. "We're so close, Peggy."

"I know," she said, a little wistful. She knew what he was going through. Throughout their marriage, she was keenly sensible of his urges to achieve, succeed, rise in the world. She did what she could to soothe him when his frustrations built to the point of breaking. Long ago she gave up trying to solve them completely. They were too many, too personal in some instances for him to be frank with her about them.

"But every time I get mad at myself I remember that St. Clair's in the same boat I am. He could just as easily have gotten an extra electoral vote as I could've, so I count myself lucky. I'm younger and stronger than he is, and we control the Congress. It'll work out. It just *has* to work out."

"It will, darling. It will," she said softly, moving over and kissing him.

"Thanks, honey."

"Look," she said, pointing to the television in the corner that had remained on the whole time in the room with the sound down. The camera image just shifted from an exhausted anchorman to the ballroom of the Pacific Arms. "They're downstairs now."

"Turn it up," said Thurston. Peggy walked over and punched a button. Thurston came over and stood beside her, looking down at the crowded ballroom packed with people of all ages who were waiting for them to appear. The picture shifted instantly to show a reporter, one of the more important reporters who followed Thurston from his first primary down to this night. Thurston knew him well, and as he listened, he appreciated the sometimes thin, sometimes thick wall that separated their professions.

". . . And now we're back here in the grand ballroom of the Pacific Arms Hotel in downtown Detroit. You all heard the announcement a few minutes ago by Terry McAvoy, Senator Thurston's press secretary, saying the candidate would be down shortly to issue a statement."

"Come on, let's not ruin his timing, honey." They smiled at each other, kissed once more, and then left the room to face the world.

Chapter 6
Sam Houston St. Clair

Governor Sam Houston St. Clair looked at his wristwatch.

Why, he wasn't exactly sure. Time seemed to be a cheap commodity tonight. All they did was sit around, wait and worry. It didn't matter if it was two, three or five o'clock. He knew *he* wasn't getting any sleep.

He sat at the end of a long table in a quiet conference room in his election headquarters in the Raleigh Hotel on South Beach. St. Clair was sequestered with his closest aides to work on the wording of his statement and to mull over the results so far. They were all gathered around one end of a long oval table with its shiny walnut veneer reflecting the overhead lights. It was out of place in the old room with its high ceilings and plaster molding. The walls had a faded look—not cheap or tawdry, but mellow and dignified.

To his left was Nathaniel Lizniak, his campaign manager. He headed one of the most successful Miami law firms and joined with St. Clair years before when they met in the state Senate. To his right was George Becker, his press secretary, a close personal friend who'd been his aide ever since he was in a position to need one. Next to Becker was Jocelyn Graham, who headed a management-consulting firm in Miami. Next to her was Howard Forbes, a prominent New York publisher, and across from Forbes sat Nathan Brooks, his personal aide and lawyer who handled St. Clair's private business affairs. His wife Sofia, who usually sat in on all such meetings, was with an interviewer in another part of the hotel. His sons, Jack and Rafael, were also in the meeting. Becker was talking.

"I think we ought to try for recounts in Idaho and South Carolina. The tallies are close in both, closer than anywhere else."

"When all the votes are in," observed Nathan Brooks, "I don't think it'll be close enough to do anything about." Jocelyn Graham agreed with a nod.

"You may be right," she said, "but I think the greatest danger lies in the Electoral College. One vote either way and somebody's going to win this baby! Just one vote either way and *somebody wins!*" she repeated heatedly, as if someone disagreed with her.

Lew Ames, a long-time aide, spoke, and at once his easy demeanor and self-confidence quieted the others.

"Guys, I'd like for you to consider this suggestion. Perhaps we might make some agreement with the other side about where this fight ought to take place. Should we opt for recounts, wait for the College to meet, or go to the House? Only if this election is as close as it appears to be, will the contest ever enter the House. Someone will have a definite advantage if there are recounts, and whichever that side is will jump at it."

There was a knock.

"Yes?" called Ames over his shoulder.

The door opened and one of his aides brought him a yellow file folder.

"Thank you, John," said Ames.

"McAvoy just announced Thurston's coming down to make his statement."

"Okay. We'll be out in a minute." John closed the door.

"What about your statement, Sam?" Forbes asked.

"Lew has something," he said.

"Yes," said Ames, pulling a piece of paper out of a folder and handing it over to St. Clair.

" 'I would like to thank you all at this time for your steadfast support throughout the primaries, in the convention, and during the campaign. It has meant more than words can express to Sofia and me. We both know that we can rely on every single one of you to continue in this struggle with us until the House of Representatives make the final decision. We pledge to you our determination to carry the fight for moderation and dignity in our government right up to the last day. To the millions of citizens who supported me with their votes, I say to you that though the decision has passed from your hands, your influence will still be the final and decisive factor in the selection of the next President. I offer you, my supporters and followers and citizens throughout the country, my heartfelt thanks and appreciation.' What do you think?"

"Strike 'by the House of Representatives,' " said Becker. "We don't know it'll go to the House."

"That's right," said Ames, and St. Clair drew a line through the clause.

"I think it sounds pretty good," said Nathan Brooks. "You don't want to say too much."

"That's right," added Becker. "It's too early."

St. Clair laughed a little cynically.

"Who ever thought election night would be too early to say anything?"

The others smiled.

"Well," said Graham, "we'd better go down the hall if we want to hear Thurston say as little as we plan to."

"They'll call us when it's time," said Forbes. "Let's go over the speech once more."

Chapter 7
No Rest for the Weary

Sofia St. Clair saw her son come through the door after an approving nod from the Secret Service agent standing there. He scanned the room quickly, with the military precision borne of his training, and caught her eye almost immediately. But she had spotted him first.

A mother's eye is quicker than any sailor's, she thought with an inward sigh.

He rushed over with the youthful energy he always had and gave her a big hug and a kiss on the cheek and then held her by the shoulders.

"*A tie!* What an election!" he beamed, his full lips pulled back over immaculate white teeth. He took his hat off revealing jet-black hair. He looked like a movie star, a Latin movie star, she thought, except when the chandelier reflected a little amber light off his deep jade eyes (like his father's).

"We're all a little surprised," she said wearily. It had been a long campaign. She leaned in close to him and gave him a tired giggle. "I thought we'd lose and go back to Flagler Hall tonight right after his speech, I swear I did."

"No," Rafael said indignantly. "The fight's just beginning."

"I know, I know," she said again, her strength ebbing.

"Where's Dad?"

"In the room next door. We'll be going down in a minute. You'll come."

"Damn right I'll come. I just wish I hadn't been on duty, you know?"

"I know."

"That damned captain of mine, son of a bitch, Skye Billings. He rearranged the duty roster just to keep me working late. He wanted me to miss all this. I just got off."

"I'm glad you got here in time. It'll make your father so happy to have you on the platform with us."

"That bastard Billings thought it would all be over."

"Your father can't use his influence with the Coast Guard. You know that, sweetheart."

"I know, but I missed all the excitement."

"I think there's plenty of excitement to go around, even now."

"Where's Jack?"

His mood darkened slightly at the mention of her stepson, and his step-brother.

"He was here a little while ago," she said, looking around.

"Shouldn't he be here with Dad?"

"Quit finding fault, Rafael." She was too tired right now to coddle him. "Jack's been here all night with your father watching the returns come in. So give it a rest."

This was like a slap across the face to Rafael, a splash of cold water. He realized he was being petty, looking to pick a fight. And this was his dad's night, and his mother's, not the time to be forcing himself onto center stage. And anyway, Jack could wait.

"Sorry. You're right. It just drives me crazy that we're about to win the Presidency and I have a Democrat for a brother."

"Other people think it's funny."

She saw his angry eyes.

"I don't think it's funny."

Why can't these boys just get along? she thought.

Her cell phone rang. She looked at the Caller ID and smiled.

"It's Ramona."

"Say Hi to her for me. I'm gonna find Dad," Rafael said, kissing her on the cheek and rushing off.

"Hi, there, Ramona."

"What do you think of all this?"

"I think I want you to buy me a drink."

"Before the speech?"

"Yes, now. We've got a few minutes."

"Come on over. I have your brand, baby."

She hung up, told her Secret Service detail chief where she was going and left with another agent close behind, walking down the corridor to another suite where the door was open. She went in and every eye turned toward her.

There was an ever so slight pause, and then everybody broke into applause and wild cheering.

Her best friend Ramona Fuentes came rushing over to give her a big hug.

"¡Ay mujer! Are you happy?"

Sofia was caught flatfooted by the question. She'd been so convinced that they were going to lose, she'd been looking forward to making the short drive from the Raleigh up to St. Clair Island where they could once and forever relax.

In fact, she was so convinced they'd lose, she forgot to be happy they *hadn't* lost.

Well, lost *yet*.

"Um, si, sure I am."

Ramona's daughter Raven came up behind her and gave Sofia a hug as well.

"¡Felicidades, Mami! I've never seen anything like this," said Raven.

"No one's ever seen anything like this," said Ramona with a dismissive flick of her wrist. "Completely unprecedented."

"About that drink," Sofia poked gently.

Ramona threw up her hands and laughed like a wild woman at a Dionysian feast.

"¡Santo Dios! This lady needs a drink," Ramona called over her shoulder to her always-nearby assistant. "Lourdes, get her Bacardi Black on the rocks, a slice of lime, si?"

"Lourdes knows," said Sofia with a nod toward the beleaguered assistant. Working for Ramona Fuentes was no easy task. Most of her "assistants" didn't last a year. What was the word "slave" in Spanish? *Esclava,* of course. But Lourdes had outlasted them all.

Lourdes was there is ten seconds with a highball glass half filled with Bacardi Black. Sofia took a welcoming sip of the dark-hued rum and licked her lips. She looked at the smiling Ramona.

"I can't believe how *good* this tastes," she said.

Ramona wagged a finger in her face and squinted with laughing eyes.

"And you thought the campaign was going to be over and you could go back to that island of yours and relax, didn't you?"

Sofia smiled and nodded. Ramona knew her every thought. She leaned in.

"I did. Between you and me, I thought this was it."

"Between you and me," Ramona whispered as she put her arm around Sofia, "so did I!"

They weaved through the crowded suite and glanced occasionally at the TV. Sofia polished off the Bacardi and as if by magic Lourdes appeared.

"Uno mas, Señora?"

"Si, Lourdes, por favor," Sofia said, handing her the glass.

"And a glass of Champagne for me, Lourdes," said Raven. She slipped away like a shadow.

Two of Ramona's daughters came charging across the room when they saw their mom was with Sofia. Raven, the older one at thirty-seven, and Antonia (only twenty-one) gave Sofia kisses on the cheek.

"You must be so *happy!*" Antonia shrieked.

Lourdes returned with the drinks.

"Yes, you live to fight another day," Raven added a little more somberly, drinking from her glass of white wine filled to the rim. *How many has she had tonight?* wondered Sofia.

She was well aware the toll a Presidential campaign took on anybody involved in one, none more so than the candidate and his wife. Sofia took an admiring look at Antonia, who still had that blush of youth and the indescribable energy that goes with it. Raven, on the other hand, had been around the block a few times, and it showed in the tense lines around her mouth and eyes, no matter how many times she had them fixed.

And yet, their mother seemed not to have aged at all. Yes, she looked her age, fifty-three, but she was master of her universe in ways her girls were not and never would be. She'd lived as hard as Raven, but still had the youthful idealism and confidence of Antonia.

She wasn't a victim of life, Ramona Fuentes, she was a conqueror of it.

Just then, Rafael came running in, glancing around for his mom. He spotted her with the Fuentes women and hurried over.

"Hey, girls! Señora Fuentes," he said, kissing all three of them, mother first. Whereas Raven accepted a kiss on the cheek, holding her wine in one hand, Antonia put her arms around Rafael's neck and gave him a hug along with a kiss.

The mothers exchanged glances and raised eyebrows.

"Oh, Rafael!" said Antonia, "you look so great in your uniform. *Tan guapo.*"

Rafael stood back and straightened his shoulders and executed a smart salute.

"Why, thank you, Miss Fuentes," he said, throwing in that dazzling St. Clair smile. He took Antonia by the hand and turned to his mom: "Nat Lizniak says Dad's just about to go down, so we need to go over now."

Sofia and Ramona finished their drinks quickly.

"I'm ready," Ramona announced.

Antonia gave a girlish laugh.

"Where's Jack?" Sofia said, looking around. "I thought he might be here with—"

"I saw them leave together," said Raven with a little more than a trace of bitterness. "Toward the elevator."

"Well," Rafael laughed, pulling out his cell phone, "Dad said he wants Jack on the podium so people can see at least one Democrat's standing behind him."

Chapter 8
Moon Over Miami

Jack Houston St. Clair and Babylon Fuentes were kissing under a palm tree down by the Raleigh pool. A Secret Service agent kept a discreet distance, looking for all the world like an unemployed shoe salesman lost in the festive surroundings. Guests splashed in the pool as political operatives clad in suits and ties moved up to and away from the busy poolside bar. But even they were laughing, smiling, enjoying the perfect South Beach weather as they realized they were celebrating *not losing* the election.

As he looked at the crowd (and listened to it), Jack realized that he hadn't been the only one thinking there was no way his dad would pull off an upset over Thurston. And while he hadn't really, the tie was even more surprising than the loss would have been. That's the only reason all these Republicans were wandering around like dizzy zombies, stunned by their *almost* success.

There'd been a never-ending rush of stories regaling a fascinated public with the fact that the Republican nominee for President had a son who was a registered Democrat. He'd been forced to give hundreds of interviews explaining why he was supporting his dad. Was he a hypocrite? His answer had been a simple one: he disagreed with his father on "certain points in the Republican platform," but not enough to support Thurston. (The truth was he did support Thurston's views more than his dad's, but he loved his father in spite of their tempestuous relationship, and he was not about to spurn him when he was running for President. Period. End of story.)

"It's kinda creepy with that guy watching us," said Babe, taking Jack's earlobe into her mouth and nibbling it.

"You used to think it was sexy," Jack leered in the moonlight, listening to the gentle breeze rustle through the palm fronds high above them. They were just far enough away from the poolside craziness to be able to hear the surf crashing onto South Beach just a few feet away.

"Yeah, well, I guess I'm a little bit over it."

"Want a drink?"

"Sure. We got time before your dad's big speech?"

"We'll make time."

Jack took Babe by the hand and pushed his way through the crowd ten deep at the outside bar. He raised his arm just enough to catch the eye of Bubba, the big barrel-chested head barman. He saw Jack was with Babe and quickly poured a double Balvenie on the rocks for Jack and a rum and tonic for Babe. Jack made his way around the edge of the bar to the service bar where Bubba filled the waiters' drink orders and picked up his drinks, which were in glasses, not the usual plastic handed out at the pool bar.

"Thanks, Bubba," Jack smiled. "Can't have that Balvenie in a plastic glass."

"Special customers only. Babe, you're lookin' babelicious."

"And you're looking bubbalicious," she smirked.

"You know, guys, that was funny for the first hundred times, but now it's really stupid," said Jack.

"Hey!" screamed an irate patron at the packed bar. Bubba flipped him the finger.

"When I get there, I'll get there."

"We'll leave you alone," said Jack. "Throw these on my tab."

"Hey, Jack, those are on me. And best to your dad. It was a close one."

"Bubba, it's *still* a close one," Jack laughed.

They took their drinks and went back to the other side of their tree, the side facing the water, away from the glare of all the pool action, the Secret Service agent keeping a weather eye on their every movement.

"What about later? You staying over?" he asked. "We can swim naked in the pool."

"There's still Secret Service."

"I'll leave the lights out in the pool."

"I drove over with Mom and Antonia."

"So what? I'll get you home tomorrow."

"Okay."

He leaned in to kiss her, the fragrant taste of rum on her tongue. He felt her hard firm breasts against his chest. The light from the full moon shone in her lustrous hair, the feminine scent of which filled his nose, making him giddy with expectation. Tonight would be a good night, the campaign be damned.

He'd been away from Babe too much to deny himself tonight.

Just then his cell phone rang.

"Fuck it," he whispered.

He pulled out his phone and looked at it before touching the screen.

"Hey, Rafael," he said. He listened. "Right. We're on our way."

Chapter 9
Path to the Presidency

Sofia St. Clair was sitting in the next room near a bar set up by a window looking out over the Raleigh's famous pool. She'd left Ramona and her daughters in the room beyond. She saw her husband come through the doorway after Graham, Brooks, Ames, Becker and Forbes and two or three others.

"Hello, dear," she said as he came over, bent down and kissed her cheek.

"Hello, how was the interview?" he asked lamely.

"Oh, you know, one of those ladies' things for *Good Housekeeping* about election night jitters. As if I'd had 'jitters' in years."

St. Clair chuckled knowingly and looked at the TV set in another corner of the room around which people in his inner circle were clustered, sitting on the floor when the chairs and sofa were filled. Gradually an ominous quiet filled the room.

St. Clair spoke up so everyone could hear him.

"Don't get so excited, everybody. He isn't coming down the mountain with an eleventh Commandment."

Everyone laughed and the tension broke.

"If he did, he'd break that one, too," said someone, and the roomful of people rocked with laughter.

St. Clair turned to the makeshift bar and poured some Pinch over ice.

"I could use this before we go downstairs," he said in a low voice. "Are you ready?"

"Umm-hmm," she cooed wearily.

"Want something?" he asked, nodding at the bar as he took a generous draft of the well-aged Scotch.

"No, thank you, dear." She beamed up at him. He turned his attention back to the television. "I had two Bacardis in the other room with Ramona."

Sofia St. Clair was proud of her husband. Always had been. Still was. As he watched the TV showing a mass of people waiting to see Frederick Thurston, she admired her husband's looks. He was a tall and powerful man in physical appearance—six-feet-two, a big forty-six inch chest, not at all fat, but strong and sturdily masculine in his bearing and manner of movement. He looked like the former Naval officer that he was, attached to General Wilson's staff in the First Iraqi War. He was awarded the DSC, DSM, a Bronze Star and a Purple Heart. She kept them on the mantelpiece at home, even when his political aides wanted him to move them to his office where more people would see them. Her husband had engaged in actual combat more times than any other officer on the general's staff simply because he always seemed to be in the hottest place at the hottest time. He'd been in more land battles, he often joked, than naval battles.

His fine dark hair was slowly turning to a silky silver. He hadn't lost a single hair, and the upright dignity of his facial features made him a most handsome man for someone sixty-four years old. His face was not lined with age marks. The deep lines were those beneath his cheeks that appeared when he smiled. They slanted down on either side of his mouth leading to his dimples. His face seemed to say to those interested in reading faces that this was a nice man who knew when to have a no-nonsense air about him and when to clap someone on the back, but a man who felt his integrity and took it seriously.

Sofia was convinced he was the handsomest governor in Florida history.

* * *

St. Clair took another long draft of the powerful whiskey as he looked away from his smiling wife and down into the lights reflected in the Raleigh pool.

A year before the election no one seriously considered St. Clair as a Presidential possibility, although there was some talk; there always is. Then, while St. Clair headed a trade mission to Beijing, a Chinese naval vessel shot down an American jet over international waters. The crew was killed. The Chinese thought it was a reconnaissance plane from the Russian fleet, which was active off the coast. While still in Beijing, St. Clair denounced the act and the Chinese gave him his passport, their thinking being that the Americans should have the same fear for the Russian threat as they had. President Norwalk angrily recalled the entire mission, which included two Cabinet secretaries, and for a week or two the whole diplomatic community held its breath for fear the two powers would sever their relations. Neither country wanted that (China held too many U.S. dollars and the U.S. needed cheap Chinese goods) and the whole affair soon went away.

Its effect on St. Clair's political future did not go away, however, and when he returned to the United States, he got a hero's welcome.

Several Republican state delegations, headed by his own, went to the National Convention tooting St. Clair's name. The primaries were largely inconclusive. The Republicans had very little new blood injected into the party during the eight years of Norwalk's presidency. Leon Coker, current Vice President of the United States, was only a year younger than Norwalk, and though he tried to capture the nomination, the delegates opted for St. Clair, who, though he was a year older than Coker, seemed years younger and even more vital and charismatic. No one believed Coker could defeat the dynamic governor from Florida, so St. Clair got the Republican nomination on the sixth ballot, in a delayed convention nominating process that hadn't been seen in generations.

The campaign was a new experience for St. Clair and his wife, because the two-term governor had never really fought to get elected before. Although on this election night he was not yet the winner, he had been able to stop what looked like the oncoming Thurston juggernaut.

For the moment, anyway.

His sons had been involved in the campaign in a small way. His older son Jack had been a bigger help than he thought he would be. His younger son, Rafael, was executive officer aboard a Coast Guard cutter based in Miami, so there wasn't much he could do. Sofia was his mother. (Jack was born to St. Clair's previous wife, a Boston Brahman named Louise Perkins, who died years ago.)

St. Clair attributed getting this far to President Norwalk's vigorous campaigning on his behalf, a strain on the man none had wished to impose. But Norwalk was a great help because he was still a popular President. He hated Thurston's pro-Chinese policy. Everyone knew it. He made it plain to St. Clair in one of their meetings that he considered Thurston a menace to the balance of power that had preserved the peace for so many years. The whole importance of Norwalk's presidency depended on the election of someone who would continue his policies.

St. Clair frankly believed Thurston would defeat him if the question ever came before the House. He'd never served in Washington except at President Norwalk's pleasure. Thurston had been elected to both houses of Congress. The Democrats had a solid majority in the House. The Democrats controlled more states outright than the Republicans did. His only really important advisor, besides Sofia, was President Jeffrey Norwalk himself. St. Clair talked to Norwalk often during the course of the grueling, tumultuous campaign. He offered much good advice and St. Clair took all he could get, including the President's choice for his running mate, Senator Robert Degraff of Oklahoma, a young man who lost his bid for the nomination but who had a national reputation. St. Clair had learned much in a short time from the foxy old President. And he knew they would talk tonight before they both turned in. He knew the old man was far from asleep even at this late hour.

Chapter 10
Lamar LeGrand Perryman

Down in Albemarle County, Virginia, in the town of Charlottesville, in a large white clapboard house with four imposing wooden Doric columns surrounded by two hundred acres, a telephone rang and rang and rang. Finally a light came on and the ringing stopped.

Lights spread into the downstairs and upstairs halls. An old butler climbed the stairs in his plaid bathrobe. At the top, he turned towards the front of the house, walked down the long, elegant hallway with its subdued sofas, Chippendale armchairs, Persian rugs and French mirrors until he came to two large doors which stood floor to ceiling, a full twelve feet high.

The butler went in without knocking and walked to the closed drapes of one of two sets of French doors that gave onto the upstairs verandah. He sashed the drapes of one of the windows allowing the full moonlight to flood into the room, picking out for him the massive bed on the other side of the room with its stately canopy high above its ornately carved four posts. The butler walked silently across the room, approached the high bed, stopping just short of the two steps used to get up into it, and reached out to touch the shoulder of the Honorable Lamar LeGrand Perryman.

He knew the old man was awake even as he reached out to touch his shoulder.

"What … is it, William?" said the old man. "… I heard you comin'." The voice was low, slow, yet distinguished and gentle.

"Telephone, suh," said William in his higher voice. "Congressman Overton—says it's impo'tant and that I oughta wake you up if'n I hadta."

"Must *be* important, then," the old congressman said, without moving, his head still wrapped in peaceful shadows while the moonlight playing through the trees danced on the white coverlet draped over his portly frame.

William went into the congressman's dressing room adjoining the bedchamber and returned in a moment with a dressing gown draped over his arm. He approached the bed, drew back the coverlet and sheet and held the gown. The old man gripped the post, as was his habit, and hauled himself up into a sitting position. He always refused help getting out of bed, saying that if he couldn't, he shouldn't by damn it, and that the affairs of state could damn well wait until he could. He stood and slipped his arms into the waiting robe. The moonlight provided all the light necessary for this business.

Perryman started out and William followed him, but overtook him going down the hall. He was holding the phone for Perryman by the time he reached the top of the stairs, where the upstairs phone was kept. Perryman wouldn't allow a phone in his bedroom.

"Thank you, William," said the old man, whose eyes were practically closed against the full light in both hallways. William retired out of earshot into another room. Perryman held the telephone to his ear and said, very slowly, "He-ll-o?"

So stood the aristocratic honorable congressman in his floor-length cashmere dressing gown as he listened to Majority Leader Niles Overton tell him the plan Thurston had divined to free the influential majority leader for other more important things prior to the assembling of Congress. As Overton talked, Perryman's hunched shoulders seemed to square themselves. But the change in posture and his suddenly alert mind did not come to him because he felt some great honor being temporarily thrust upon him. That was nothing to him. While Overton finished, Perryman's mind was already forging ahead to the floor of the House and other matters secreted inside his somewhat large head.

"Now it … wouldn't do," he drawled to the majority leader, "to have two speakers die in the chair one right after t'other." They both laughed a little.

"I'm not worried, Lamar. I know you'll do just fine. We'll be getting together on this thing later. Thurston said he'd call you tonight, so you might want to wait up."

"I'll do that, Niles, now don't you fret," the old gentleman said.

"All right then, Lamar, I'll let you go."

"Good night, Mr. Majority Leader," said Perryman good-naturedly.

Overton hesitated just a second and Perryman caught it, just enough to show how badly Overton really felt about not being in a position to argue in his own behalf for the speaker's chair. But he replied with a little laugh in his voice meant to please and flatter Perryman.

"Good night, Mr. Speaker."

If anything could be said about the venerable representative from Virginia, it was that he could never be flattered, and almost never pleased. He was the only one who knew it, though. Publicly he pretended to be flattered often enough, but he even more publicly pretended to be pleased. He seldom was in the latter case and never in the former.

Congressman Perryman put down the receiver, rewrapped his dressing gown and tied it back again. When he spoke his voice was not slow and sleepy, as it seemed to be to Overton.

"*William!*" he snapped out sharply. The butler came through a door instantly.

"Yessuh?" answered William.

The old man started pacing, with hands behind his back and his belly leading him on by a foot, addressing William as he might a general staff preparing for battle.

"What time is it?"

"Fo'clock, suh."

"I'll stay up, William."

"Yessuh."

"Roust out Becky to get my breakfast. Juice, coffee, toast this morning."

"What kind o' jams, suh?"

"What? Oh, blackberry, I s'ppose – no, bring me some of that marmalade the British ambassador gave me."

"Yessuh."

"Light the library."

"Yessuh."

"I'll eat in there."

"Yessuh."

"I'll take calls from now on."

"Yessuh."

"Lay out a suit of clothes."

"Yessuh."

"Roust out Tyree. Tell him to get the car ready. I'm goin' to Washington this mornin'."

"Yessuh."

"You and Tyree will come with me. Becky stays here 'cause we'll be back."

"Yessuh."

Perryman stopped.

"William?"

"Yessuh," said the butler, looking back with interest at Perryman. He liked to see the old man excited.

"William, you are looking at the next speaker of the House of Representatives and not just speaker for a couple of weeks."

"Lor', Mr. Perryman, I'm proud fo' that."

"No need to be, it doesn't mean much to most people down in Washington. Not much glory in a thing like this. I won't be speaker long, William," he said with a glint in his eye, "but I have a hunch, yes, William, a mighty solid hunch, people will remember I was speaker when the time comes I'm not again."

"Yessuh."

"All right, light the library and get on about it."

William "lit the library" and then ran around waking Becky the cook and Tyree the chauffeur. Then he went upstairs to arrange the congressman's wardrobe before going down to his quarters to get together his own.

Becky got out eggs, bacon, grits, coffee, bread she'd baked fresh the day before and a jar of Tiptree Tawny Orange Thick Cut Marmalade made by Wilkin & Sons, Ltd. (a little on the bitter side for her taste), and started making breakfast for Perryman and the two other servants.

The congressman's light breakfast was ready very soon and she took it into the library where he was at his desk with his feet propped up, thinking. She scolded him for eating so little and said she put some bacon on the tray. She stayed and watched him eat, fussing around him.

"You didn't eat that bacon," she pointed out, standing arms akimbo as he blithely looked the other way. *"Eat that bacon!"* she demanded.

He looked at her sharply and extended his arm slowly and with imposing majesty towards the library door before he snapped out at her.

"Woman, get out of here *and leave me alone!"*

"Not till you eats all that bacon!" she snorted back at him, not moved a bit by his imperious command. *"Eat!"*

He rolled his eyes to heaven.

And then ate the bacon.

Tyree went into the garage and took the old Lincoln limousine to gas it up for the congressman's trip later that morning.

Finishing his breakfast to Becky's satisfaction, Perryman climbed the ladder as she went away with his tray. He was looking for a certain reference book. He was just down when the telephone rang again. He snatched it up eagerly, but answered in a slow, sleepy drawl.

"He-ll-o?"

Thurston's voice was slow, steady, respectful.

"Hello, Congressman—Fred Thurston. I'm sorry to wake you up, but I guess you've already heard from Niles."

"Yes, indeed I have, Senator. He has informed me of your strategy and I concur wholeheartedly. He'll be of much greater value to you in the weeks before Congress convenes."

"That's what I was thinking, Lamar. He'll have to make some trips for me I couldn't ask you to make."

Perryman was not flattered. He knew he wouldn't have been called on to make the trips anyway.

"I'm glad I can be of some help, Senator," said Perryman politely.

"And you can be … Lamar. You'll have to keep a tight rein on the House and the caucus after you're elected speaker. It might not be easy. Niles and Stan are coming here tomorrow to plan strategy."

"Senator," injected Perryman, "I will be happy to jump on an airplane and come myself, if you think it necessary."

He knew Thurston would not think it necessary.

"It's nice of you to offer, Lamar," replied Thurston, "I wouldn't want you to go to the trouble, but I appreciate it. Niles will fill you in later."

What he meant, thought Perryman, was that he not only didn't think his advice meant much, and never had, but that he didn't think his influence was that substantial. His influence might not be now, he thought, but his power soon would be.

"Thank you, Senator. I'll look forward to hearing from you and the majority leader, then, after you have deliberated."

"Thank you, Lamar. Good night."

"Good *morning* to you, sir."

"Yes, it is morning, isn't it?"

Perryman heard a click as Thurston disconnected. He slowly lowered his receiver and replaced it in its cradle. His mind was working faster than it usually had to.

Perryman wiped the palm of his hand across his mouth, removing the thin film of sweat on his upper lip. He realized that he would have to make some basic decisions rather soon and he wanted to be prepared to make them for the benefit of the country. He was asking himself questions Overton and Thurston thought he'd answered for himself long ago. Perhaps, thought Perryman with a slight smile, they thought he was far past the age when men made all their final decisions lest death should catch them short.

Perryman returned to his books and pressed a button on his desk that brought William to the library door.

"Yessuh?"

"I'll dress now, William."

"Yessuh." William turned and moved slowly up the stairs to prepare to dress the congressman. Perryman himself went back to his ladder and fetched down some books he wanted to take with him to Washington.

In an hour he would be dressed in his habitual winter worsted suit, heavy topcoat, Homburg, gloves and walking stick, the picture of a distinguished elderly gentleman.

But I've still got some poison in my fangs, he smiled to himself as he moved slowly up the stairs.

Chapter 11
Matt Hawkins

It was five o'clock in the morning in Jackson, Wyoming, and in the pre-dawn light that filtered into the room, Matt Hawkins was making love to his wife, Sue.

The snowy November landscape cast a pale, muted half-white light through the heavy-hanging drapes. The light played across the muscles of Hawkins's body, creating quiet rippling shadows among the bulging sinews of his back and thighs. The well-defined muscles shifted as he lifted for each new thrust, and beads of sweat rolled off his back. The prickly sweat between his legs lubricated his movements. The small of his back was a puddle of darkness. The room was quiet but for their labored breathing. He was thinking now of the time they did it behind a waterfall roaring off a mountain in the Teton Range. They'd been in college then.

His head was on her shoulder, turned away from her face. He stopped momentarily, lifted himself on his elbows and kissed her smooth shoulders, sweaty neck and lips.

There was no mistaking the fact that Matt Hawkins was handsome and his wife beautiful. It was something all the people agreed on, whether they voted for him or not. He was twenty-nine years old and she was two years younger. He had dark, curly hair that gave him a boyish attractiveness that brought out more than a maternal instinct in women. His complexion was such that he retained the slightest tan and looked exotically dark to the bleached faces of Wyoming, used to long and bitter winters. He was healthy and warm looking, having what many women voters called a cozy personality.

Many women who went to Moran High School with him remembered that "cozy" personality and the times they curled up with Matt in front of warm winter fires in isolated mountain cabins. Many wished then and now that they could have caught Matt and married him, but he always moved on to someone else, even though he never hurt anybody when he left. No one he ever made love to could say she'd been hurt by Matt Hawkins. Most were happy for the experience and didn't try to argue when his restless nature asserted itself. Matt knew he never hurt people and was very proud of the fact that he could bed most of the women he wanted without causing any trouble when they broke up. He never gave them false hopes. The word "love" was never used.

Sue Williston, with her gleaming dark brown hair and light hazel eyes, was the one who finally got him. She met him at the University of Wyoming, she studying English, he preparing for the law. They married in his first year at law school, but even now they had no children.

He kissed her lips again. It was getting lighter outside.

"Happy?" he asked, still inside her.

"Um-hmm," she purred.

"About this?" he said, flexing.

"I thought you meant about the election," she said, laughing slowly, "not the e-*rec*-tion."

"Well, it rhymes. You *might* be happy about both," he said. "After all, you are married to the new representative from the state of Wyoming."

"Succeeding defeated William R. Crampton," she intoned. "Well, you're not the congressman from Wyoming yet, hot shot," she pointed out.

"Well, not yet. But *soooon*," he leered. "Crampton's a lame-duck till I get sworn in next January."

"I never liked him."

"I didn't either, at first, but I didn't know him then. As the campaign went on, I liked him more and more. Kinda hate to see him go."

Crampton had been the single representative from Wyoming for many, many years. He'd been considered untouchable by anyone in either party. Republicans never fought him and many people thought Hawkins was just plain lucky to beat him in the Democratic primary. The combination of his youth, looks, obvious legislative talent and his law background and reputation in Jackson and Cheyenne pulled it off even without campaigning in every part of the state.

Hawkins once said to an aide that if the voters could see him, *not on television,* but in the flesh, he knew he could win. Throughout the campaign, Crampton refused to debate him publicly, knowing Hawkins had the kind of magnetism that would turn Crampton into Nixon—and Hawkins into Kennedy. So the main push in Hawkins's campaign had been to show himself in person to as many voters as possible.

It worked. They were electrified by his warmth, outgoingness and youthful brashness. Especially the women. One poll of two thousand women in Cheyenne found only three hundred fifty two who wouldn't vote for him.

"You're losing it," said Sue.

"Oh," said Matt, bringing himself back and forgetting about old man Crampton.

Sue could tell his heart wasn't in it as he pushed deep inside her, again and again, a soft, wonderful grunt coming from him each time. But his body was certainly there, and when she thought about it, that mattered more to her—his body. That's what attracted her to him in the first place. Yes, she was attracted to the other things in the man, but his body was what kept her. For her part, without sex there wouldn't be much else to their relationship. For a man like Matt, for whom sex was always available when he wanted it, other things she didn't even consider mattered more. And though Sue was beautiful, and had a gorgeous body, she fell behind him in those "other things," such as ambition, glory, power and money, all of which Matt thought about endlessly. To the point of boredom, in her opinion.

And now they had to go to Washington.

Matt propped himself up on his arms, looking at Sue as they made love, but her eyes were closed and she was breathing heavily, about to come. She always closed her eyes just before. Now she clawed his back, and he laid his head back on her shoulder, away from her face, scarcely feeling her fingernails in his tight, agile back, thinking how, over the years, the emotion had slipped away from their love-making, one fuck at a time. He knew they wouldn't be together forever. So did she. He wouldn't be surprised if he came home one day and found a note on the refrigerator.

They finished. He lifted himself on his strong arms and rested beside her, running his index finger across her sweaty forehead, down her nose and onto her neck. The house was hot, sealed against the snow and cold outside, and they were both lying in pools of sweat. He pulled the top sheet up over them gently, the coolness of the cotton soothing his hot skin and muscles.

"We'll have to start packing this week," he said.

She rolled over on her side to face him, though she could barely make out the contour of his face in the half light.

"It's going to get pretty tense in Washington, isn't it?"

"Sounds like it—from the way things are shaping up."

"Will it involve you much?"

"Nobody even knows I exist outside of Wyoming."

"You never know," she said.

"I know," he said, moving closer to her and kissing her again. He slipped his arm under her head and held her to him.

"Get a little sleep, Mrs. Congressman."

She closed her eyes.

But, try as he might, as exhausted as he was after all he'd been through, he was wide awake as his mind raced ahead to think about the wonderful challenges that lay ahead.

Chapter 12
The Last Call

Governor St. Clair had been on the phone most of the night. He was extremely tired after he returned to his suite from the blaring convocation of trumpeting voices and noise that had been the ballroom's sendoff. He only talked to three people, however: Congressman Duncan Olcott, Robert Degraff and Jeffery Norwalk, in that order.

At 3:30 A.M., St. Clair called Minority Leader Duncan Olcott of Illinois. His secretary answered and said Mr. Olcott was on another line and had two calls waiting but that she would tell him St. Clair was on the line. In a moment Olcott answered.

"Hello, Sam?" Olcott said in a rush.

"Yes, hello, Dunc."

"I've been waiting for your call," said Olcott, "I've already called all my part of the delegation. All my people are steady. I've been working on theirs, but they're afraid to talk to me before they meet with Healy. He's called them all to Chicago tomorrow, but I'll keep trying to get at 'em."

"Thanks, Dunc," replied the candidate, thinking now about the troublesome mayor of Chicago, Edward Healy, a real force to be reckoned with in Illinois, and Olcott's bitter enemy. "But what are the chances it all might be settled in the College?"

"Don't know. I'll tell you this, Sam. The people that vote against their party on this one, whether it's in the College or the House, and I don't care which way their state voted, are going to be crucified. I don't care who they are or what they feel on the issues. We've got to make sure all the Republicans in the House know exactly what's expected of them. In this kind of fight we're looking for bodies and everybody knows it."

"I guess you're right. Then you think it'll go to the House without much doubt?"

"I'm pretty sure of it. Even though it hasn't happened in over a hundred years. Since we've only got twenty states for sure, we've got our job cut out for us. It won't be easy, Sam, you know that."

"Yes," said St. Clair. "What do you suggest I have my people do?"

"I'll fly over to see you tomorrow, Sam, and we'll meet with your people. We need files on every congressman and we'll have to divide them up and somehow go to them all—the crucial ones, that is."

"All right, Dunc. I'll see you tomorrow. You talked to Frank?"

"Yes, I called Frank an hour ago. He'll come with me." Frank Holtzman was the minority whip from Waterbury, Connecticut.

"All right, Dunc. I'll see you tomorrow."

"Fine, Sam. And Sam…"

"Yes, Dunc."

"Don't you worry, boy. We'll pull this one through somehow. I'm not sure how just yet, but we'll pull it through."

"All right, Dunc. See you tomorrow. Good night."

"Good night."

Then he talked to the junior senator from Oklahoma, Robert Degraff, his running mate. Degraff said his own House delegation, though Republican, was in some doubt because of the enormous influence of John Fulton, who controlled the four-to-two Republican majority in the delegation.

Fulton personally hated both Degraff and Norwalk. Degraff said he was still working on his fellow Republicans, but that they were afraid to commit themselves without first talking to Fulton. He said he would fly to Miami the next day. St. Clair was very pleased with his running mate. He was serious, hard working and idealistic—and just thirty-eight.

Then St. Clair placed a call to the White House.

"This is Governor St. Clair. Is the President awake?"

"Yes, Governor. He left instructions to put you through immediately."

Chapter 13
The Oval Office

President Jeffrey Norwalk stood looking out the windows on the south side of the Oval Office into the dark but glittering Washington night. The winter having killed all the leaves on the trees between the White House and the Washington Monument, the President could see the monolithic slab of rock pointing like a pin-prick to heaven, towering over the city with undiluted brilliance and unmolested majesty, the harsh spotlights seeming to coat the monument not with a garish night time make-up, but with an invisible shroud of honor and dignity. He knew the same kind of lights were shining on the White House, making it look, even in the night, like an undefiled object, clean and pure in its neoclassical simplicity, overpowering in its quiet strength, sturdy and immovable in times of shifting factions and restless masses, representing to many millions of Americans who thought they were as pure, unadorned and inviolable as the great big house where they put their best man every four years, a kind of self-image.

Early in his administration, when he was in the Oval Office late one night and looked out the windows as he was doing now, the brilliant lights that flood the building were located forty yards from his office windows, pointing straight at him. They blinded his vision and he couldn't see outside clearly. And they made him restless. To him the lights immediately symbolized (so briefly had he been in office) the attention of the world, so powerful was their focus on him and his new home. The very next morning he ordered them to be shifted so as not to obstruct his view of the city at night.

He turned away from the south windows into the Oval Office itself, which was very dark, illuminated only by his small desk lamp. He walked over to the French doors on the east side and looked out into the Rose Garden whose now absent blooms, so healthy and life-restoring in the spring, he would not see again as President: perhaps never again, he thought. Former Presidents seldom returned to the White House, much less the Rose Garden. He took pleasure in that garden more than any other part of the grounds. He'd planted bushes there himself, and recalled one occasion when the wholesome dirt covered his hands, and the sudden rush of reporters when someone spotted him with a couple of staff members and the secretary of state on their hands and knees. He mused that perhaps it was his love for growing things that urged him on to become President. It was his habit to look at nations and peoples as flowers and plants. They had to be cared for, nurtured, fertilized, watered, protected from winds and frosts, or from great heats.

He knew that was all a lot of bullshit. It was his lust for power that made him President. And his full appreciation of power that made him a good one. He had no apologies.

How strange, he thought, returning to the Rose Garden, that the President of the United States should have only this small, neat garden in which to stroll when the kings of France had had the acres of formal gardens at Versailles.

Of course, he thought, there *weren't* any more kings of France. Maybe the Rose Garden wasn't so bad, after all.

He opened one of the French doors, eleven and a half feet high, and swung it outwards, bringing in a sudden rush of cold November air that chilled him more than he thought it would. He was getting old, he thought: seventy-three and he felt each one of those years. He was a long way from the forests of Ohio where he grew up and camped out on many a wintry night.

Stepping out onto the small portico outside the French doors, Norwalk felt the winds whip round his head, mussing his gray hair. He walked down into the Rose Garden, feeling the frost crush under his feet. It was cold, he thought again to himself, as though having to remind himself that he was freezing.

He'd been thinking all evening about the inconclusive election, and finally made up his mind a little earlier what he would do about it.

His mind was overburdened with the election, with Frederick B. Thurston, his enemy, and Sam Houston St. Clair, his protégé. He was skipping around in his mind from thought to thought, impression to impression, sensation to sensation, trying to judge his life, weigh the effectiveness of his two terms as President, Russia, China: their feud and totally irreconcilable destinies.

He forgot them for the moment.

Norwalk was lost in his daze, though his vision was as sharp as the air was bitingly cold. He felt numbed, however, as though his eyes were not connected to his brain. He looked around the garden as if seeing it for the first time. It was all clear but strange. He walked out of the Rose Garden, around the West Wing to the front. Only a few cars were cruising Pennsylvania Avenue at this late hour, slowing even as they passed to stare at the place he'd called home the past eight years.

He walked toward the fence that surrounded the grounds. The curving drive sloped slightly away from him to one of the two car entrances on this side of the White House. Two guards were chatting together in the warm guardhouse. Norwalk stayed out of the light by walking beneath the bare branches, strong and outstretched, of a tall ancient oak tree.

Walking down to the fence, he took one of the bars in his hand and held it. He felt slightly dizzy. The iron bar was freezing and seemed to sear his hand with the cold.

Just then he heard rapid footsteps and turned towards the guardhouse and drive, his hand coming off the bar.

Running towards him at a fast clip were the two gate guards and several White House police and soldiers who were running down the drive as fast as they could, their greatcoats flapping in the light breeze. He was startled and for a moment physically afraid, having forgotten where he was. He felt the threat of assassination every President lives with day-to-day flash through his mind until he remembered where he was. In an instant he was fully surrounded and several flashlights made him close his eyes. He faintly saw some of the light reflect off the cold metal of drawn revolvers. There were two or three gasps from astonished guards.

"Mr. President," said one of them. "We had no idea it was you. The Secret Service didn't tell us you would be out walking tonight—and unescorted."

There was a hint of irony in Norwalk's voice when he spoke.

"No, because I didn't tell them. I'm sure the sensors on the door I opened have them running down here right now."

And he was right. From the direction of the Rose Garden half a dozen agents were running toward them frantically. They slowed down when they saw the President with an escort.

"I'm sorry, Mr. President," said an Army officer who had run down from the White House portico with the others. "We have to take every precaution. Back to your stations, men," he ordered crisply. The flashlights were lowered and the men went away. The officer came to attention and saluted smartly.

"I'm sorry that you were interrupted in your walk, Mr. President." He hesitated. "Would you permit me to offer you my coat, sir? You aren't wearing anything and it's very cold out tonight. Less than twenty degrees."

Norwalk was quite aware of the cold now that his stupor was gone.

"That would be very kind of you, young man." The officer rapidly slipped off his coat and draped it over the shoulders of the old President.

"I'll go back now. Don't know why I stumbled out here in the first place. Must have given the others a shock, and you, too," he paused and chuckled. "What's your name, son?"

"Benson, sir."

Norwalk looked at his insignia.

"Well, Lieutenant, thank you. You are very efficient. I don't know you, do I? Are you new here?"

"Yes, sir. I've been here about three months."

"Three months," mused Norwalk.

Both men were thinking the same thing: the President always welcomed staff members of the White House to their new jobs. But such occasions were group affairs and were set up only several times a year. While the individuals remembered everything about the informal chat they had with the President, he himself could not be expected to remember every individual.

"Three months," Norwalk mused again. "I'm sorry, Lieutenant Benson, I don't remember you. You will understand, I'm sure."

"Of course, Mr. President."

Norwalk smiled at the young man's serious face and ramrod back. Then he lightly laughed.

"Will you do me a favor, Lieutenant Benson?"

"Certainly, Mr. President."

"Stand at ease."

"Yes, sir," said Benson, relaxing as much as he could.

"Why don't you walk me back to my office, Benson. You and my detail here can protect me from any would-be assassins leaping from the trees."

"I'd be delighted, Mr. President," said Benson, smiling.

They walked back the way Norwalk had come.

"Will you be missed at your post?"

"No, sir. The captain won't mind when I tell him where I was."

"No," remarked Norwalk, "I suppose he won't." They went into the Rose Garden where Norwalk stopped.

"Do you like flowers, Benson?"

"I haven't had much time for flowers, sir," replied Benson, thinking it over and using the perfect excuse for any question.

Norwalk smiled broadly, then laughed. All his laughs seemed to grow out of slowly broadening smiles.

"Do you think I'm a busy man, Lieutenant?"

Benson flushed with excitement at being there in the Rose Garden talking about flowers with the President of the United States in sub-twenty degree weather. He could only answer one question at a time.

"Sir, you're the busiest man in the world."

Norwalk held his finger up in mock admonishment.

"There then, Benson, let that be a lesson to you. If I, the President, can take time to smell flowers and even to plant and pot one now and then, it follows that a young lieutenant can do the same."

Benson blushed and held his head down, saying, "Yes, sir."

The President turned to the Secret Service detail.

"The rest of you can return to your posts. I won't be slipping out again. Not tonight, anyway," he added with a twinkle in his eye. "Come to my office with me, Benson," said Norwalk on an impulse as he shot up the portico and through the still-open French doors.

Chapter 14
The Keystone File

Once inside the Oval Office, Norwalk looked over at Benson.

"Close the door."

The lieutenant closed the door and the heat quickly returned to the room. Norwalk took off Benson's coat and handed it to him and sat behind the desk.

"Sit down, will you, Benson?"

Benson looked around him into the dark shadows in the corners of the quiet room.

"Thank you, sir," he managed to say as he sat down.

"Tell me, Benson have you been in here before?"

"When I first came here they gave us a tour."

"Not since then?"

"No, sir." He paused. "Are you sure I'm not keeping you from anything, Mr. President?"

"Of course, my good man. You wouldn't be here if you were. I was just thinking about the election, the result, and waiting for a phone call."

Benson looked startled.

"You have to wait for a phone call?" he asked. The tone of his voice was unmistakable. The President doesn't have to wait for anyone to call him—*anyone*.

"Well, it's not that pressing a phone call, and I had to do some thinking for myself, Lieutenant."

"I'm sorry, Mr. President, I didn't mean to pry."

Norwalk laughed again.

"I'm sure you didn't, Benson." Norwalk paused. "Tell me, what did you think of the election results? Be honest."

"Well, Mr. President, I voted for Governor St. Clair and I'm sorry he didn't win."

"Well, he hasn't *quite* lost, Lieutenant."

"No, Mr. President."

"But then, he hasn't quite won, either."

"Yes, Mr. President."

"Why did you vote for St. Clair?"

"Because I don't like the Chinese, sir."

Norwalk raised his eyebrows and said, almost to himself, "That's pleasantly simple."

"Excuse me, Mr. President?"

"Never mind. Do you know what's going to happen with this election?"

"I've been on duty since eleven o'clock, Mr. President, and from what I've heard from the captain, it's going to go to the House of Representatives."

"Do you know anything about all that?"

"No, sir. I never thought what would happen if there was a tie. It's never happened before, has it?"

"Well, a long, long time ago, but not quite under these circumstances," he said, looking away from Benson into the dark shadows in the room, looking into his past, his own and the nation's. "It happened a long, long time ago," he said softly.

"To which President?"

"To Thomas Jefferson, for one."

There was a long pause as both men thought the same thing: Why was the President talking to an inconsequential first lieutenant about a matter of such great national importance?

The console buzzed. Norwalk touched a button. "Yes?"

"Mr. Slanetti is here, Mr. President."

"Very good. Send him in."

"Ah," said Benson with a slight smirk.

"What's that mean, Lieutenant?"

"Oh, nothing, Mr. President. Just that I know his name. It's hard to remember all the people who work for you. We have to memorize them."

Norwalk laughed.

"I have the same problem you do, Benson."

"I know he's your aide for Congressional liaison."

"Right you are, Benson, right you are. And he's going to be earning his salary the next few weeks."

The door opened admitting a flood of white light from an outside corridor and a man in his early forties walked in.

"I've looked over those files of mine you asked about, Mr. President," said the man as he walked into the room, the white light behind him, looking rather curiously at Lieutenant Benson as he came over.

"Yes, thank you, Phil," said Norwalk. "Lieutenant, this is Phil Slanetti, my— well, you already know, of course."

Benson jumped up quickly and faced Slanetti.

"Yes, Mr. President."

"Yes, very good, Lieutenant," said Norwalk. "Well, I think that will be all, Benson. You may return to your station."

"Yes, Mr. President. And thank you, sir," said Benson, coming to full attention. He performed a neat about-face and left through the open door Slanetti used.

"Have a seat, Phil," said Norwalk. Slanetti took Benson's chair. "You're probably wondering what in God's name he was doing here."

"I *was* wondering," Slanetti offered.

Norwalk laughed again. "I just bumped into him a minute ago when I was outside walking."

"Outside *walking*, sir?" asked Slanetti, skeptically.

"Yes," said Norwalk. "Even Presidents take walks. Now tell me about those files you've been keeping."

"They are up-to-date, Mr. President. The only information they lack is what I will add when the freshmen members come to Washington. But for all existing members, they are quite thorough."

"You mean you've been keeping them up-to-date all this time?"

"Yes, sir. Just a habit, I guess. Once I have a file, I like to keep it updated until I deactivate it. You never said to deactivate them."

"I guess I didn't."

"No, sir."

"Actually, I forgot all about them right after the election," said Norwalk. "I'm waiting now for St. Clair's call. Mind staying with me a little while?"

"Of course not, sir. Happy to."

"Good," said Norwalk, reaching for his pipe. He filled the bowl and then lit the tobacco, saying out of the side of his mouth as he puffed to catch the flame, "You can smoke if you like, Phil. But you don't smoke, do you?"

"That's right, I don't, Mr. President. But thank you."

"Hmm," said Norwalk, puffing contentedly. "My wife would have patted you on the back, Phil. She hated my smoking. I finally gave it up for this damn thing, but since she died I've grown to like it."

"Yes, sir," Slanetti said unemotionally.

Norwalk caught the lifeless tone in Slanetti's voice. A real functionary. A minion. But you needed people like him in a job like this. They *did* things. Things you couldn't do.

They sat for a few minutes, Norwalk quietly rocking in his large, high-backed, black leather swivel chair, blue smoke rising and clouding the light, Slanetti observing the man he served, his head safely covered in shadows as he sat just outside the small circle of light cast by the old desk lamp.

It was at this point that St. Clair placed his call. There was a clear, and in the quiet room, sharp buzz as a light registered on the President's console. He leaned up and punched a button activating the speakerphone.

"Yes?" he asked.

"Governor St. Clair is holding, Mr. President," said a White House operator.

"Put him through." There was a familiar click and Norwalk knew the line was open. "Hello, Sam."

"Yes, Mr. President. I hope you weren't asleep. I'm sorry for being so late with this call."

"I understand the reasons, Sam. Tell me what your people think."

"Well, they're pretty upset, as I guess we all are. I've talked to Dunc Olcott. He's called Frank Holtzman and we're going to have a meeting out here tomorrow to look over the roster of the new House and see how things stack up."

"They feel pretty sure that it'll go to the House, then?"

"That's what they think, sir. Dunc is sure of it. I myself am afraid of an elector swinging the decision one way or the other, and as long as they aren't controlled, that could as easily happen against us as for us."

"That's what I've been thinking, too. I may have an answer for that, if what I have in mind works out. And I think it might. But listen, you meet with your people, make your decisions about the various members involved in a contest in the House. When you feel sure about the individuals that may cause trouble, on either side, you get back to me and we'll set up a meeting. We've got a while before the new Congress comes to town and there ought to be time to do something."

"Very good, Mr. President. I'll do just that. What have you got in mind?"

"Well, you just leave that to me. When you get your list, you call me up."

"All right, Mr. President. I'll get back to you."

"Good, Sam. Give Sofia a kiss for me, will you?"

"Yes, indeed, Mr. President."

95

"Good night, Sam."

"Good night, Mr. President."

Norwalk punched a button and leaned back in his chair. Blue smoke once again clouded the yellow light from the old-fashioned desk lamp, a gift from his late wife, whose smile shone out from his favorite photograph of her at the lamp's base. (She was precariously balanced high atop a disgruntled camel in front of the Pyramids, a side trip they'd made on a state visit to Egypt.)

"Well, you heard that, Phil. What do you think?"

"I think you're going to want me to work with Governor St. Clair's people on this."

Norwalk sat forward in his chair and put his hands on his desk, looking into the darkness around Slanetti.

"Partly. You are going to work *for* St. Clair and his people, not necessarily *with* them. I'm not quite sure how I want this thing handled. You can understand that. This is going to be delicate work. Very delicate work, indeed. I haven't asked you what kind of information you have in those files, but I can imagine. Some of the stuff the whole town knows, but nobody talks about. I'm sure you know which is which."

"I've made myself acquainted with all the details, yes sir. Even some of the most scandalous items could not be used because everybody knows about them already and the member involved knows he'd be protected by the silence of his friends and associates. But there's enough material for your purposes, I think, Mr. President."

"For *my* purposes, Phil?" the President asked, raising his eyebrows.

"For the purposes … at hand, sir."

"Considering the turn of events, I'm glad to know you've been keeping those files. I'm also glad we didn't have to use them four years ago."

"I know what you mean," said Slanetti.

"I'm sorry we have to use any of it at all, Phil."

"I can understand that, Mr. President."

Norwalk leaned back again and thought back to his own campaign for reelection four years back. He was under considerable pressure in that election. The Sino-Russian enmity had had a particularly violent flare up, but that was nothing to compare to today's dangerous climate. There was a well-funded third-party candidate of extremely dangerous potential that Norwalk was afraid might conceivably take enough electoral votes to throw the election into the Democratic Congress. Without question, had that happened, Norwalk would have lost the election. So he had a young aide of his, fresh from the Justice Department, this same Phil Slanetti, work up an in-depth file on the private lives of every congressman and senator, including anything that could remotely be used publicly or privately against the member's reputation, his career, his family, his business interests, his dignity, welfare, etc. It was an ambiguous assignment in its description. Norwalk never had to use the files, and only he and Slanetti knew of their existence. He hadn't even told his campaign manager.

Norwalk now realized Slanetti had in his possession some of the most highly inflammable information the government had anywhere. It was the kind of information no one liked and of which everyone, in varying degrees, was afraid. The question was: Would they be afraid enough to vote for St. Clair against their wishes, against their consciences, senses of personal integrity and constitutional duty? *Of course they would,* thought Norwalk, cynically, *they're politicians.* There were damn few of them that weren't crooks in one way or another by the time they got to Washington, and the ones that weren't were soon converted by the piles of cash coming out of the expensive leather briefcases of K Street lobbyists.

"Yes, very delicate, indeed," Norwalk repeated. Slanetti waited patiently. "Here's what you do, Phil."

"Yes, sir."

"Sam's people are going to meet with Olcott. They'll do what we can't do right now, which is make a canvas and find out where the members stand today. When they know I'll have Sam come down here. We'll—you and me—we'll have a look at this list. Then we'll just see what they can do on their own. I'll work with them in the open, pressure as many members as I can in the conventional sense. I don't want to have to use you if we don't have to."

"If I may say so, Mr. President, they won't be able to do it on their own."

"You're right," Norwalk sighed, puffing away.

"If I may, Mr. President, I'll draw up my own estimate of the way I think the House will vote so that when Governor St. Clair brings his list, we'll have them to compare."

"Good idea, Phil. Do that. It could be interesting to see who's not on whose list."

"Yes, sir."

Norwalk hesitated, something he seldom did.

"How *good* is this file, Phil?"

"Good, Mr. President, very good," said Slanetti with the same unemotional voice he always seemed to use but which struck home to Norwalk as it never had before.

"Then it's very, very bad, Phil."

"You could say that, Mr. President. Or you could say it's very, very good."

"Let me just give you a name—a file you're bound to know. What have you got on, say, Niles Overton?"

"The majority leader is so-so. But even his hands are dirty."

"He's wanted to be speaker for years. Much on him?"

"There is one thing that could ruin him completely. He's not a silent partner, exactly, but more of a beneficiary, in a land development company in Minnesota. Most of the money is funneled through his ex-wife, and she gets over two hundred and fifty thousand dollars a year off the company's developments."

"Is that illegal?" said Norwalk.

"Not until you find out his ex-wife—well, not her exactly, but a shell company controlled by her—started invoicing the company just before it bought large tracts of land along the eventual route of a new interstate highway that went through the state, something Overton knew about in advance because of his position on the House Public Works Committee."

"That's big enough to drive him out of office."

"That's what I assumed, Mr. President."

"How about, oh, someone like John Fulton of Oklahoma? Bob Degraff will probably have a hard time with his own state if it comes to the House. Fulton hates me and he hates St. Clair."

"Fulton is easy on the surface, but he'll be hard in fact. He hates Robert Degraff, that's common knowledge. But he's guilty of extortion. Because he's ranking member on the House Interior and Insular Affairs Committee, he's had plenty of opportunities. He's been accepting great sums of money for years for his influence and support of the oil lobby. But it's not directly from the oil lobby – it's from the equipment and parts manufacturers that the money gets filtered, from subsidiaries all based abroad, not here in the U.S. Those parts companies have a much smaller profile than the big oil lobby. He's smarter than most, though. He keeps it all in an unnamed, numbered bank account on the Isle of Wight. It's unreported, untaxed and very illegal."

"John Fulton, huh?" said Norwalk with a slight smile on his face. "How much has he got over there?"

"It's hard to know exactly, sir, but easily more than twelve million."

"My God, Phil. There are no surprises in politics, you know?" Norwalk said rhetorically as he got up and walked to the windows on the south side of the office and looked towards the Washington Monument. He turned back to Slanetti who rose and faced him.

"How did you find all this out, Phil?"

"In Overton's case, it wasn't easy. Well, none of them are easy. I checked his IRS file. It showed nothing, so I checked his wife's file. Nothing again. The partners' files. Nothing out of the ordinary. Run-of-the-mill private sector multimillionaires like most of the hogs eating the pork. But if you look at the uncles, aunts and nephews of Overton's *ex-wife*, not his current wife, you hit pay dirt. They're all millionaires many times over. And it all comes from Overton. Even his current wife doesn't know about any of his illegal activities. And when you check the company's transactions and compare them to Overton's voting record in his committee, it all works out."

"And bingo, just like that," said the President quietly.

"Yes, sir," said Slanetti unemotionally, bland as sand.

"How'd you track it down?"

"Not so easy. I have informants in most lobbies that I can count on when I need them. I was aware of the payments to Fulton in recent years, though I have no full retrospective accounting. At any rate, I knew what he was getting. It was never reported, I checked that first. Then it was just a matter of time and looking before I found out where he kept it. I have some discreet contacts in Switzerland, which led me to the Isle of Wight. A little money works wonders with regard to information, Mr. President. Then I checked the deposit amounts on the Isle of Wight—I was able to get those for the past few years—with the amounts I had been informed he was paid. Bingo. That's where he keeps his money."

"So you also have files on Overton's ex-wife, Fulton's people, their aunts and uncles and partners?" remarked Norwalk as he returned to his desk and sat down. Slanetti remained standing.

"Yes, sir. I have expanded the original concept somewhat, just to make the files complete."

"Expanded it?" Norwalk's eyes showed extreme interest.

"Yes, sir. I investigated any person who could be connected in an illegal way with the person I was interested in. You can often go through someone to get the man you're after. I also made investigations of selected persons on our own side, purely for defensive purposes."

"I see," said Norwalk. He banged his pipe upside down in the ashtray and refilled it. "It's a sound assumption, Phil. It's good to know what others can use against you, even your friends."

"Just my thinking, Mr. President."

Norwalk was tempted to ask Slanetti one certain question pertaining to his own life, his "forgotten" past, if a President can have one, but he assumed that if no one else in the country knew certain things, maybe even Slanetti didn't. He looked sharply at Slanetti, but as the aide for congressional liaison was standing, he could just barely see his face, which was above the circle of light on the desk. He did ask something, however.

"Funny the media doesn't dig deep enough to find more of this stuff, don't you think, Phil?"

"Not really, sir. Maybe in the seventies and eighties, but now it's all about drugged out rock stars and whether they're wearing underwear. The media is pretty much in control."

"It's amazing when you invite a network anchor to a state dinner for the French President how tame the questions get at the next interview."

"Exactly, Mr. President. Of course, you have to throw them a fish every now and then, even one of your own."

"When they've been attacked, anyway, and bleeding from a wound."

"Yes, sir. Unfortunate, but it happens. The people think that person's just a bad apple, the rest of the apples are okay."

"So your investigative system is better than anything the media can throw at Congress."

"It is unexcelled, Mr. President. Newspaper reporters, network reporters, insurance company investigators, even most police, don't have the resources of private information that I have at my disposal."

"What resources?" asked Norwalk. It was the only stupid question he ever asked in his life. Even Slanetti took the liberty of thinking so.

"The federal government," replied Slanetti.

Norwalk blinked, feeling incredibly stupid. Maybe it was the late hour.

"Yes, well, we'll talk more about it later," said Norwalk. He rubbed both his eyes with his hands. "God, I'm tired," he said, standing up. "You can go on with your work, Phil. I appreciate your thoroughness, and even more than that, your loyalty."

"Thank you, Mr. President," said Slanetti. He then turned and went to the door.

"Oh, Phil?"

"Yes, Mr. President?"

"What are you planning on doing after we leave office?"

"Haven't decided, Mr. President."

"Right."

Slanetti closed the door behind him.

Norwalk watched him go and then touched a button on his console.

"Yes, Mr. President?"

"I'm going up to bed now."

"Yes, Mr. President. Good night."

Norwalk went towards the door that led down the corridor to the elevator. A guard was standing by the elevator.

"Good night, Mr. President."

"Good night, Alfred," he said.

Oh well, he thought as he went up to the second floor living quarters, bad as all this was, he felt completely justified in using the information Slanetti gathered simply because of the volatile nature of the Sino-Russian conflict. Nothing was more important to Norwalk at this point in his life and career than the certain election of Sam Houston St. Clair to succeed him. He was willing to suspend the laws of the land in order to acquire the information needed against the opposition. He saw that Slanetti had already done most of the footwork necessary and already compiled what he needed.

He knew he could sleep a little late tomorrow. The Russians and the Chinese ought to be quiet for a few days owing to the inconclusive election results. Chances were they were as startled about the developments as everyone in Washington was. The elevator doors opened and he walked down the hall to his bedchamber. Lonnie, his night usher, came out of another door and opened the door to his bedroom.

"Long night, Mr. President, yes?"

"Long night, Lonnie."

Minutes later, as Norwalk fell asleep, his mind slipped back to earlier in the evening when he'd been watching the results come in on TV and realized a tie existed in the Electoral College.

He'd called Slanetti, who was working late in his office, when he first remembered those old files. He'd asked if Slanetti still had them.

"Oh, yes, Mr. President. You never told me to deactivate them, so I've been keeping them up-to-date all these years. They're quite thorough."

Perfect, Norwalk thought. *What great good luck!*

"By the way, Phil, what was the name we gave those files?"

"A very fitting name, Mr. President. You said you'd had one term to construct a firm foundation on which peace could prosper and you desperately wanted to have another term to put the last piece in place so the whole structure would hold."

"Noble words, Phil."

"Yes, sir. Code name is the Keystone File."

Chapter 15
The *Mirta*

Paco Agular knew there was trouble when he felt water on his flip-flops suddenly rise to his ankles just seconds before a muted alarm sounded in the forward section of the *Mirta*.

José Asanza, what you might call the "captain" of *Mirta*, came rushing back through the narrow passageway.

"Paco, you and Ramos pull out the Zodiac. Get it above and be ready to inflate when I give the word," he said in Spanish.

There was a quiet panic among the five-man crew. Everything a crew did on a narco-submersible was done in quiet.

"What's leaking?" Paco asked.

"Fuck if I know. Looks like the exhaust valve, where it's bolted into the hull. We've had trouble with it before."

Most narco-subs were scuttled after a single mission. (A single load could fetch $200 million wholesale, and the sub only cost a million, sometimes two. A minor cost of doing business.)

But *Mirta* had avoided that fate because she was a top-of-the-line ship (she was named after the Cartel boss's *abuela)*, had made seven round-trip voyages from Colombia to Florida and Mexico, and was in great shape, except for the leaky exhaust valve that even now was spewing water into the ship like something that reminded Paco of the water gushing into *Titanic* about to rise over Leonardo DiCaprio's head when he was chained to that pipe.

They had been running along at 15 knots, even if the seas were a little rough right now, but basically taking it easy after a harrowing trip up from a remote part of Colombia's Caribbean coast near Soledad all the way to an uninhabited island that was one among dozens off the coast of Little Torch Key in the middle of the Coupon Bight Aquatic Preserve in the Lower Florida Keys. It had been pitch black when they unloaded over ten tons of cocaine into a series of go-fast boats that took the product to safe houses and trucks waiting at various spots along U.S. 1.

The cargo they were transporting back was what interested Paco more than the coke they'd delivered. They were bringing back $65 million in small U.S. notes: 5s, 10s and 20s, plus 50s and a fair share of C-notes.

The public always focused on the drugs imported into the U.S., without wondering how the cartels got the money those drugs generated *out* of the country. Part of it was money laundering. A lot of it was money laundering. But a lot of it just had to be hauled out like so many sacks of trash. And what better way to make use of a submersible that would otherwise head back home empty?

Paco inwardly grew more frantic as the water rose another foot up to his knees and he dwelled on the thought of $65 million sinking to the bottom of the ocean out in the middle of nowhere.

Paco pulled the Zodiac out of the aft section of the ship and pushed it ahead to Ramos.

"Pull it up forward and I'll be right there," he said, leaving Ramos to manhandle the craft forward while he dipped back to the tight little bunks that formed the sleeping quarters when the crew was off watch. He found his small caliber Beretta M418 and slipped it into his pocket, hurrying back forward before anybody noticed. He didn't know where he would end up, but he wanted the comfort of having the small Beretta with him. A later model, it carried eight rounds, plus the one in the chamber.

Paco and Ramos quickly hauled the Zodiac up to the hatchway as the *Mirta* broke the surface. While José and another crewman desperately worked to staunch the broken seal on the exhaust pipe, Paco and Ramos waited by the hatch.

José yelled up to them.

"Open the hatch and inflate the boat!"

They pushed open the hatch, seawater dripping down onto their heads. Paco was first out. He hauled up the Zodiac bow first until it was all the way up and resting on the flat surface of the sub.

He glanced around him in every direction, but saw nothing. Ramos followed the raft out of the hatchway and together they inflated the craft and tied it off to cleats on the port side. A 55-horsepower motor was hoisted up to them and they fastened this to the stern board and made it ready.

Glancing up at the sky, Paco saw the faintest trace of light in the east. It would be dawn soon enough.

Paco could feel *Mirta* settling fast. It wouldn't be long now. He stuck his head down through the hatch.

He could hear a litany of the most vile curse words known in the Spanish language coming from the fanatically stressed-out captain.

"You need me, José? What can I do?"

José's face appeared in the dark passageway below. He shook his head.

"It's no use. We're sinking." He turned to the other crewmen with him. "Vamos! Ahora!"

The other crewmen scrambled up the hatchway ladder as Ramos untied the line and hopped into the Zodiac.

Paco looked back down into the darkened interior.

"I'll get our exact coordinates so we can pass them along," said José, disappearing for a half minute.

"Start the engine and hold steady," Paco told Ramos.

The crewmen rolled over into the Zodiac as Paco leaned back into the hatchway looking for José, who suddenly appeared with a stack of money bound in tight plastic wrap. He pushed it up to Paco, who took it and tossed it over his shoulder to Ramos as José crawled out of the doomed *Mirta.*

"Expenses," said José, forcing a smile as he came out of the ship. He handed his satphone to Paco before pulling up two cans of fuel for the Zodiac.

"How far can we get with this much gas?" Paco asked.

"We got lucky, Paco. We're in the Dry Tortugas, not far out at all."

"That *is* lucky," said Paco, absorbing all that José said without actually saying it.

"The last position I took about an hour ago put us south-southeast of Fort Jefferson on Garden Key. If we head north-northwest, we could hit Long Key and then we'd be safe."

"But we're only eighty or so miles from Cuba. Don't we have enough gas to get there?" The last place Paco wanted to go was Cuba, but he thought he had to make the suggestion, if only to prove to José why he was the captain and Paco wasn't.

"I don't think so. The Americans will have to let us go. The Cubans, you never fucking know with them. A Zodiac this nice would be a big addition to their Navy," he laughed. "In these seas, the gas won't last long climbing swells. And if we run out of gas, we go where the current takes us, and that could be anywhere. Too many sharks in the Florida Straits."

"Yeah."

"Without *Mirta*, the Americans have nothing on us." He looked over to the other crewmen. "You all have your papers?" Everybody nodded. They carried their papers in their back pockets as a hedge against something like this happening.

José pulled out his compass that glowed in the dark and looked at it.

"I'll take the rudder," said Paco, taking the compass from José.

"OK, amigo. Hold on to my satphone. When we get under way, I'll give the coordinates to our central so they'll know where *Mirta* ended up. These waters aren't fifty feet deep. They ought to be able to recover the money in a couple of months, when we're long out of the picture. Steer a course north by northwest and in an hour or so we should see some land. Go very slowly so we don't use much gas."

Paco moved back to switch places with Ramos and settled in by the engine, holding the compass in one hand. He stuffed José's satphone into the pocket holding his Beretta.

"OK, everybody," José addressed the crew, facing forward. "It's bad what's happened here, but it happens. The good news is we're not going to die like our friends last month off Mexico." Paco knew he was referring to another sub that went down without a trace a hundred miles off Puerto Vallarta. "And when we get clear of the Americans and get back to Colombia, we'll all get paid."

Paco laughed to himself. These jokers would only get $10,000 for the trip, hardly the princely sum he'd been expecting until *Mirta* took on water. He looked over his shoulder as José explained to the crew where they were and what would happen once they reached shore. He watched as *Mirta* settled lower and lower into the water and then, with only a little gurgle to mark the moment, slipped silently below the warm waters of the Gulf of Mexico, taking $65 million in cold hard cash with her.

José pulled up the big stack of bills secured by plastic wrap and ripped it open.

"There's no evidence of anything, so everybody put some money in your pockets. We'll need it later to get home. They can't prove anything."

After everybody had money tucked away, José tossed the rest of the plastic bag full of cash overboard, shaking his head as he did so.

Paco looked up as the Zodiac topped a broad swell and thought he saw a light flash before the Zodiac dipped into a trough. At the top of the next swell he saw it again.

"José," he called out. "Dead ahead. A ship's light."

José stopped his yakking and whipped out his Barr & Stroud field glasses and took a look.

When the trough pushed them up to the next swell, Paco rode it for a few seconds so José could get a better look. That was all he needed. Paco had seen it, too.

"That's no ship, Paco. That's Fort Jefferson." José turned back and looked into his binoculars. Over his shoulder, he said, "Bring her up to half speed and let's get some shitty American coffee for breakfast."

Paco looked over his shoulder at the spot where *Mirta* had just sunk. He quickly glanced at the gas level in the tank and at the precise reading of the compass. He stood up to get a sense of the distance from dead reckoning and took special note of the time on his wristwatch.

He brought the speed up to half as José came back towards him.

"Give me the satphone. I'll tell our people the coordinates and then we'll ditch the phone so the Americans can't trace anything."

"Ah, you have the coordinates?" Paco said redundantly, almost trying to sound slow in the head.

José tapped his shirt pocket and smiled.

"Just wrote them down."

In the three or four seconds it took Paco to reach into his pocket and pretend to fumble around looking for José's satphone, a hundred things went through his mind all in a flash, so he only had the fleetest of moments to decide to pull out the Beretta instead of the satphone and shoot José right in the middle of his forehead before he even got his eyes open wide in recognition of what was happening.

José took the shot to the head and fell overboard as the other crew members turned around in shock. Paco pulled the throttle back to idle and shot each of the crew in the head before they even had a chance to rush him.

Once they were dispatched, he got some speed up and circled back to find José floating face down in an up-rolling swell. He caught up with him, brought the engine back to idle, and grabbed the man by his hair. He leaned over and with his other arm, took José by one of his legs and hauled him into the Zodiac, fishing around in his shirt pocket for the piece of paper with the coordinates.

He took a waterproof flashlight from the kit and examined the coordinates over and over until he could recite them perfectly.

Stuffing the paper into his own shirt pocket, he repeated the coordinates over and over in his mind as he heaved José back over the gunwale and into the rough waters of the Gulf. Each of the other crew members followed in short order. He took care to splash some seawater all over the front of the Zodiac to rinse some of the blood away, but he couldn't get it all. He didn't want the blood to be too obvious to the park rangers when he landed at Fort Jefferson.

Taking a look around the Zodiac and thinking that everything looked as shipshape as it was going to look, he went back to the idling engine and brought the speed up to full throttle as he made for Fort Jefferson.

Along the way, he tossed the satphone over the side. The thing that most impressed him about the loss of the submersible off Puerto Vallarta was how furious the higher-ups had been that the crew hadn't sent along the coordinates when the ship went down, making it impossible for them to attempt to recover the cargo. It was a total loss.

If they didn't know the coordinates of *Mirta*, then they couldn't recover the $65 million resting easily in her hold in less than fifty feet of water.

Up ahead he saw a great number of lights now as the silhouette of Fort Jefferson came into view. He also saw a powerboat approaching the Zodiac at high speed.

He'd been reciting the coordinates in his head even since reading them. At this moment, he took the slip of paper out of his pocket, looked at the coordinates to verify he had them firmly memorized, and ripped the paper into shreds and tossed them overboard. As soon as he recognized the logo of the National Park Service on the side of the patrol boat bearing down on him, his Beretta went over the side as well.

Paco smiled.

"Ahoy there!" he yelled out in perfect English.

The boat circled him and a ranger called out through a bullhorn to find out if he needed assistance.

"Yes, our ship sank!"

"We are coming alongside!" came the reply.

Paco cupped his hands together to shout back, showing them that he wasn't armed.

"OK, thanks!"

He sat back and waited for them to approach.

He hated the name Paco. In Spanish, it was a nickname for Francisco. Because he really wasn't Paco, or Francisco, or Agular. He was Laurencio Duarte, an undercover agent for the DEA who had just come up with a plan to make a whole lot more money than the piddly couple of million he expected to get from his secret deal with Omer Flores.

Chapter 16
Morning Thoughts

Dawn was just breaking as Lamar Perryman's limousine pulled onto Arlington Bridge. Perryman was glued to the cable news channels on the TV monitor in his car. Everything was focused on rehashing the evening's news, over and over again, hour after hour. Perryman hoped the Constitutional scholars the networks had hauled out of bed were earning overtime aplenty.

The only new item was an announcement that the lame-duck President Norwalk would address the country at 1 P.M. that afternoon.

Perryman had been surprised to get the call that would make him speaker in the next session. And he fully understood why Thurston wanted to keep Overton busy applying pressure to the undecided members. Perryman could conduct the largely ceremonial functions of speaker while Overton counted votes in the cloakroom and worked behind the scenes.

The Virginia congressman was even more impressed that Thurston had made this call after Perryman refused to endorse any candidate in the election. Perryman had answered all the questions from the press—not to mention members of his own party—with his position that the Sino-Russian conflict was a confusing one and he wasn't sure which path was the best to follow. Thus, which candidate to endorse?

Secretly, and no one knew this, he fully supported the Norwalk-St. Clair pro-Russia policy.

He deeply distrusted Chinese ambitions over the long haul. They were hoarding American cash by the tens of billions, and had been for years. They were ever-increasingly a major importer of goods to the U.S., costing millions of Americans to change livelihoods as all the lower paid jobs went overseas to sweatshop factories or to illegal immigrants at home in the face of an inability of either party to develop a comprehensive immigration policy. In fact, as old as Perryman was, he couldn't remember the time when there *had* been a cohesive immigration policy.

All those iPads and iPhones sold by Apple? Made abroad. Perryman remembered a meeting he attended in San Francisco in which President Norwalk asked Apple's senior management if there were any way their products could be manufactured in the U.S. rather than abroad.

The CEO had shaken his head. "Those jobs aren't coming back, Mr. President." Perryman actually thought it was nearly impossible to *have* a cogent immigration policy. After all, hadn't we stolen the country from the Indians? Who's to say who *really* belonged in America?

Well, while Apple's products continued to sell like crazy in America, they certainly weren't made here.

What child (or adult, for that matter) could look under a Christmas tree and not find that almost all the gifts had been "Made in China"?

Like the wars in Iraq and Afghanistan, the Middle East peace process, the economic doldrums in Europe, solutions to the really important issues kept rolling over from one administration to the other, from one party to the other, back and forth, on and on, *with no forward motion coming from any source*. It frankly disgusted him that no one who finally achieved power would exercise it plainly *except* to benefit the short-term special interests that got a President elected in the first place. And then reelected. And this he thought was true of *both* parties. He thought it ironic, though also emblematic, when he first heard that Clinton and Bush had the same tailor: only the special interests were different. The cut of the cloth was the same.

Also, the Chinese stash of American dollars always gave them an upper hand in trade negotiations with the U.S. No trade envoy in Republican or Democratic administrations had ever made any progress with the Chinese in terms of equalizing trade agreements. *The Chinese are just plain smarter than we are*, thought Perryman, and the threat, never spoken but always implied, that the Chinese could flood the currency markets with American dollars, was always in the back of the minds of Washington policy-makers. The U.S. was just plain cowed and out-maneuvered by the Chinese—that was Perryman's view.

Perryman picked up his walking stick and tapped on the window between him and Tyree. The window came down.

"Pull over to that Starbucks on the corner, Tyree, and get me one of those *latte* things I like."

"You know what the doctor said about those coffees, Mr. Perryman."

"You and Doctor Rembert can discuss the deleterious effects of the caloric content of my coffee at my funeral, Tyree."

Tyree smiled and pulled over. He eyed the pocket edition of *Merriam-Webster's Collegiate Dictionary*, twelfth edition, that he kept on the seat whenever he drove the congressman. He wanted to look up that word, *dele-, deleterious*, whatever it was. He pulled the car to the curb and touched the flasher button.

In the back seat, Perryman reviewed the history. The Russians were now preparing to invade China as a *defensive* measure, and Perryman believed the Russians had every reason to be as frightened of Chinese intentions as Norwalk, St. Clair and Perryman were. After all, it was the *Chinese* that precipitated the whole crisis by building that damned canal to divert water away from Kazakhstan and Russia. Water without which Russian crops would wither and die, throwing half the country into famine within a year.

The car roared to life as Perryman settled in with his calorie-rich six-dollar cup of coffee.

"Be mindful of the potholes, Tyree," he cautioned. He sipped his coffee, but not through a straw. He was brought up never to use a straw. Never been one in his house. His mother would have slapped his face sideways if she ever saw him drink through a straw. "So common," she used to say disdainfully whenever she saw someone do it. He still marveled when he saw fools at a White House state dinner ask the waiters for straws for their Diet Cokes!

Question uppermost on his mind now was how he could use his newfound power to advance the Norwalk-St. Clair position over that of Thurston and his own party. Having been sidelined for so many years, his new position might give him just enough marginal power to make a difference.

What a grand idea that is, he thought. He remembered that segment that always ended Aaron Cross's NBC broadcast. It was a series called "Making a Difference."

That's me, God damn it! Finally making a difference!

The old man smiled and he held his coffee cup well away from his fine overcoat as the car hit a nasty pothole.

"Sorry, Mr. Perryman," said Tyree.

"That's all right, Tyree," Perryman smirked as he brought the Starbucks cup back to his lips. "I saw it comin'."

Chapter 17
Scrambled or Fried?

The phone rang in Jack Houston St. Clair's bedroom and he snapped it up on the third ring, before it went to voicemail. He glanced at the clock on the end table: 7:05 A.M.

"Oh, Jesus," he moaned.

He was still incredibly groggy after getting home last night a mere three hours ago. He and Babe had thought about just *sleeping*, they were both so exhausted after the rigors of the campaign, but once they lounged around in the hot tub next to his pool for half an hour, they came in and couldn't keep their hands off each other. But, as hot as their passion was, it was quick, and they both fell into a deep and thorough sleep.

"Yeah?"

"Sorry to wake you, Jack," said his father, "but we're getting up early to do a little strategy, so if you feel like it, bring Babe over for breakfast."

"OK, but I need thirty or forth minutes just to see if everything works," he said.

The elder St. Clair laughed.

"You're telling *me?* I'm the one with the sore joints. You're the ex-SEAL, don't forget."

Yes, he was the ex-SEAL, all right, but he didn't feel like one just then. Babe wanted to sleep in a little longer, so he hauled himself out of bed and crept toward the bathroom where he threw himself under the cold jets of water that he knew would revive him. (Although, he thought, even "cold" water in Miami was often 75 or 80 degrees.)

He came out and threw on a robe and went out into the Game Room overlooking the 9th green that separated his modest house from the grand Flagler Hall on the other side where his dad lived. The waters of Biscayne Bay sparkled as they caught the early morning November sun, like so many millions of diamonds being bounced around on a turquoise blanket.

Jack smelled the coffee and turned just in time to see Gargrave coming into the Game Room from the kitchen carrying a pot that he placed on the bar.

"I saw the caller ID, sir, and thought you might be wanting this."

"Thank you, Gargrave. You're reading my mind, as always."

He'd known Gargrave for years, when they worked together in the service. Jack had been a member of the super-secret SEAL Team 9, the one SEAL team (there were ten teams altogether) the Navy never admitted even existed. While he still wasn't happy about the *way* he left the SEALs, he was glad now that he was out of the military.

Gargrave had been a member of Squadron M in the Special Boat Service (SBS), a covert element in the Royal Navy. Their units shared a secret assignment in Afghanistan.

When Jack left the Navy, Gargrave followed him and became a sort of butler or major domo to Jack, who needed someone not only to manage his house, but to help run St. Clair Island as well. He was also a big help to Jack as a backup operative running the St. Clair Agency, Jack's detective agency with a meager three employees. When those rare occasions came along when Jack took a case, Gargrave was an invaluable asset. Ex-military men could be very useful in such work.

"Breakfast, sir?"

"No, I'm going over to my dad's to eat."

"Very good, sir. And the lady?"

"Let her sleep. When she gets up, she'll probably come over to the Hall. Now we have this damned tie, we're playing everything by ear, even breakfast," he smiled as he took a long draft of the coffee.

Jack went back down the hall and quietly slipped into his dressing room where he got some clothes on and headed back out through the Game Room's sliding glass doors.

He glanced at his three boats tied up at the dock, at a uniformed soldier standing on the quay with his rifle, looked across the Bay toward Miami, being sure to check out the 9th green (they were supposed to cut it yesterday, and hadn't) as he crossed to Flagler Hall.

Henry Flagler (one of John D. Rockefeller's original partners in Standard Oil), whose Florida East Coast Railway had started first Jacksonville, then went down to Palm Beach, and then Miami before crossing the Keys to finally end up extending all the way to Key West, had built the 55-room mansion as one of his winter homes in Florida in 1902. It was a masterpiece of Beaux Arts architecture.

Flagler died in 1913. In 1914, a Force 4 hurricane devastated Miami, leveling almost everything in its path, gutting Flagler Hall, but leaving its "bones" fully intact.

One of Jack's ancestors had washed ashore during the hurricane and taken shelter in the huge house and weathered the storm there.

When Flagler's widow saw the ruined mansion, she sold it to Jack's ancestor for a song (along with the island itself). All St. Clairs since then had been raised on the island. The island was the foundation of their fortune, as it kept giving back money as each parcel of the island was developed over the generations. The key to the St. Clair fortune was that you couldn't buy a lot on the island. You had to lease it from the St. Clairs. Flagler Hall had been turned into a clubhouse once the golf course was built, and the current head of the family lived on the upper floors while the lower floors were used as the clubhouse.

The St. Clair Island Club was the most exclusive club in Florida, one of the most exclusive in the whole world. You couldn't apply for membership: you had to be invited. There were only 400 members worldwide.

After passing the Secret Service detail out in front of the house, he went around to the southeast side of the Hall where an open patio led up to a glassed-walled room often used for breakfast because it caught so much of the morning sun. He saw Sofia and his dad just walking out of the house and taking their seats. Felipe the houseman was pouring coffee, American for his dad and Cuban for Sofia.

Jack nodded toward a Secret Service agent standing guard a slight distance from the patio.

"Bet you're glad you got assigned to my dad, Ralph," Jack said, extending an arm toward the Bay and taking in the whole beautiful gorgeous panorama.

"Yeah," Ralph laughed, "I could be up in Detroit with Thurston."

"Where it's snowing," Jack laughed.

"Yeah, where it's snowing."

Jack opened one of the French doors as Ralph spoke into his mike to report to his central that Jack was joining the Governor.

Sofia and Sam looked up and smiled tired smiles.

"You guys look as tired as I feel," he said, nodding to Felipe. "Café con leche, por favor, Felipe," who nodded and went off to get the coffee.

"What a night, huh?" said his dad.

"I thought it would be over," said Sofia. "One way or the other," she shook her head, draining the small cup of Cuban coffee, a *colada*, dark and intense. "Una mas, Felipe, por favor."

"The worst thing about being a politician is having to do those God damn morning shows like *The Today Show* and be on your toes—or look like you're on your toes—when what you really want to do is fall into bed and get some sleep."

"He's turned down twenty interviews already," said Sofia, taking up the demitasse cup that Felipe put in front of her.

"More like fifty!" Sam boomed. "They can damn well wait a few hours. Nothing's going to happen right away. We're all frozen, deadlocked."

"So what's it looking like this morning?"

"I've got the whole senior team coming over in about an hour to do a little strategizing. Want you to sit in on it."

"Right."

Felipe hovered.

"I'll have two poached eggs, bacon and sausage," said Sam. "Sofia?"

"Una tortilla de cebolla, Felipe. But just half of one. I'm not that hungry after last night."

"Si, Señora. And you Mr. Jack. Scrambled or fried?"

Jack either had his eggs fried or soft scrambled.

"I think I'll have the other half of Sofia's onion omelet. Those are good."

"Yes, Mr. Jack."

"But I'll have bacon and sausage like my dad. Extra of both."

Felipe nodded and left the room.

"So, Jack, before all the shit hit the fan, what were you planning to do today?" asked his dad with a booming guffaw.

"I was going down to the Bankers Club for lunch. Got a new client."

"Why you keep dabbling in that low-rent detective agency is beyond me, Jack."

"I don't call it 'dabbling,' Dad," said Jack, his anger rising. "I call it a 'job,' and I have the luxury to do it because Grandpa left me a big enough trust fund so I don't have to jump every time *you* bark."

"Boys," said Sofia quietly.

"Sorry," said Sam.

"Me, too," said Jack.

But they weren't. Each felt the other was right.

Jack was always surprised how hard Sofia worked to make his relationship with his dad easier. She was like the lubrication that kept their two powerful gears from grinding each other down into inert black dust. And she wasn't even his mother.

"Where is Rafael today, anyway?" Jack asked. "I saw him last night, but then he disappeared."

"He had to work this morning."

"That Skye Billings really puts him through the ringer ya-know? Sure you couldn't ask Norwalk to get this guy transferred to the Aleutian Islands or somewhere?"

"I'd love to, but that kind of thing is delicate, especially when it's no secret that Captain Billings doesn't get along with his executive officer."

"Who just happens to be your son."

"Rafael can take care of himself," Sofia said. "Skye Billings is just jealous of Rafael, that's all there is to it."

"He thinks Rafael's been coddled because of his family, but that boy works hard at everything he does," said the Governor.

"He's got to prove himself more than Skye does."

There was a slight pause at the table. Jack saw Sam and Sofia looking outside. He followed their gaze and saw that they were looking at the miracle of beauty that Biscayne Bay could sometimes be on a winter morning in Miami, when the sun was just right, there was a nip in the air and the water sparkled.

"God, whatever else, we're lucky," said Sam.

"We are," Sofia echoed.

"You know, as bad as things are in the world, with all its problems and trouble, I still look on this time as the 'good old days.' Whatever happens, whoever survives will look back and remember how really wonderful it actually was."

Jack smiled as he looked at his dad. He noticed Sam had reached over and was holding Sofia's hand as they looked out over the water.

Dad's right, he thought, *Life is good.*

Chapter 18
Getting Home

Omer Flores and the other passengers on American Airlines flight 875 from Tegucigalpa to Miami were allowed to deplane when it was announced that there would be a two-hour delay in San Pedro Sula, the second biggest city on Honduras after Tegucigalpa. He was hot, dirty and tired, having been delayed for two hours already and stuck on the tarmac in Tegucigalpa.

So now I'm four hours behind, he thought, pissed off.

He pulled two phones out, put his "official" DEA phone back in his pocket and used the other one to text Derek Gilbertson in Miami: *Running 4 hrs. late. Call when I get MIA.*

He hadn't heard from Gilbertson the day before—when he'd expected to—about the funds transfer from Dade International Bank (DIB) to his two banks—the Bank of Jamaica and the British bank in the Caymans—where he kept his personal accounts and where he thought, by this time, his share of the money would have shown up. He was a little nervous that it hadn't, and he wanted to know why.

All he knew was that Gilbertson kept putting him off, that there had been a funeral a few weeks ago and that the "paperwork" was not getting through the pipeline fast enough to please everybody involved.

Especially Omer Flores.

At the time, Flores had been in the jungle collecting another $20 million from traffickers to push through that pipeline and hadn't had a lot of time to deal with "paperwork" problems. Uppermost on his mind was the often delicate task of just staying alive, something always on the mind of an undercover DEA agent.

It hadn't been easy for Flores to work his way up to the level where he was now, a level where he could command a respectable piece of the action of the laundered funds he'd been pushing through channels for the DEA.

And now that he was in a position to bank a chunk of Big Money, he was a little anxious to see that the "process" went smoothly. Which meant that he had to keep a watchful eye, not only on his pal Derek Gilbertson, but also on his colleagues at DEA. It was almost as nerve-wracking as looking over his shoulder at the Sinaloa and Zetas cartels.

"Damas y caballeros, se les informa que habrá un retraso adicional de una hora para la salida del vuelo 875 de American Airlines, rumbo a Miami …" came over the speakers.

Damn! He'd have to cool his heels for still another hour in San Pedro Sula. Would it ever stop? Sure it would. When he had put away five or six million offshore, left the DEA and disappeared without a trace. He knew how to disappear. He just wanted to make sure he had enough money to make it worth his while.

Chapter 19
Before Dawn

It was hours earlier in Wyoming and Matt Hawkins was wide awake and staring at the ceiling while Sue slept peacefully, a soft purr rising and falling with her breath.

He'd come quite a long way in his twenty-nine years, if he did say so himself. He couldn't wait to get to Washington and the new adventures that waited for him there. He thought back to his youth growing up in the Grand Tetons, son of a dad who was a ranger there, a dad who'd taught him about the sanctity of nature, about the bond that existed between the natural world and the world of man.

He thought back to the first girl he'd taken into the mountains on a camping trip when he was still a freshman in high school. She'd wanted to see an elk, or so she told him. But they both knew all either of them really wanted was to get laid. She was two years older than he was, and that was fine with him. They did see an elk, maybe two.

It wasn't until college that he met Sue. She was ambitious, maybe even more so than he was, which was saying something. He was drawn to her edgy personality, her sharp wit, pushy insouciance, bold ideas.

In addition to which, in bed she was a wild animal. Sex, sex, sex. Never was there too much sex for Sue Williston.

Things had tapered off in that regard, however, as the pressures of her highly successful law career grated against his own ambitions politically. But she had been the model politician's wife, was a part of his inner sanctum of advisors, the Hillary Clinton to his would-be Bill. The main difference between Sue and Hillary was that Sue wanted power without the crap, influence without the posturing. No baby-kissing bullshit for Sue Hawkins. No pandering to political gabbers at nursing homes that wasted your time. She wanted big money and wanted to make it representing interests that needed access to power. She wanted to be the power behind the elected officials, and she was quite frankly a little puzzled when Matt first came to her about running for old man Crampton's seat. She didn't come right out and say she thought he was nuts, but he could see it in her eyes.

"Well, it's your life," she reminded him.

By this time, of course, they'd long since made the move from Jackson in the northwest part of Wyoming to the capital of Cheyenne in the far southeast corner.

When he made up his mind to run against Crampton, he called the congressman's office and made an appointment. Everybody on Crampton's staff knew who Matt Hawkins was—the promising young lawyer who was the talk of the town. He'd met Crampton at several functions, but they weren't chummy.

"So, what can I do for you, my friend?" was how Crampton opened the meeting that day a year ago.

"I wanted to drop by personally to tell you I'm going to run against you in the primary."

"Oh, really?" Crampton replied without missing a beat. He did, however, get up and go to a bar against the far wall where he poured himself a drink. "Offer you something?"

"What are you having?"

"Oh, George Dickel—it's a sour mash whisky."

"I'll have what you're having."

"Ice?"

"I'll have what you're having."

Crampton brought the two glasses over and handed one to Matt before taking his chair again.

"Now, what in God's name do you want to run against me for?"

Matt took a sip of the Dickel and made a face. *"Whoa!"*

"You look more like a Scotch man, really," said Crampton. "Got a taste for this stuff from a Virginia congressman, Lamar Perryman."

"Chairman of the Ways and Means Committee."

"Yes, a powerful congressman."

"Well, the reason I want to run against you, Mr. Crampton, is that I don't think you're ever going to retire and give somebody else a shot."

The seventy-two year old Crampton laughed at this, a big belly laugh.

"You may have a point, young fella. Ever since my wife died a couple of years ago, I've found that my life in Washington is more rewarding than what I'd have back here if I did retire." Hawkins didn't say anything. Crampton went on. "No one has *ever* challenged me in a primary contest, you know that?"

"I do. That's why I think it might rustle up a little excitement," Matt smiled ingenuously.

Crampton had to admit he liked the guy, but he didn't let on.

"I'll fight you tooth and nail, you know that?"

Hawkins got up and placed his now-empty glass on the congressman's desk.

"I do know that. But I have a feeling: *this is my time*."

Crampton got up and they shook hands.

"Thanks for the courtesy of coming over to tell me personally."

"My pleasure, Congressman," Matt said, smiling a brilliant smile that soon the voters of Wyoming would come to know all too well.

* * *

They got to know that smile well enough to win Hawkins the primary, but only after a spirited defense by Crampton, and only by a margin of two percent.

Crampton came to see Hawkins at his office after he'd lost the Democratic primary.

"Sorry I don't have any George Dickel to offer you, Mr. Congressman," Hawkins said with a laugh.

"That's all right—I didn't think you would, but there's a saloon near your office that I'm particularly fond of, if you have a few minutes to spare an old congressman."

"My time is yours, sir," Hawkins said, getting up and following Crampton the three blocks to a

Cheyenne watering hole where they took seats at the bar.

"No hard feelings?" Hawkins asked as he lifted a glass of Scotch (Johnnie Walker Red and a splash) to touch the lip of Crampton's glass of Dickel on the rocks.

"Not at all," said Crampton, taking a long sip of his whisky. "But since you won by such a *small* margin, and since the Republican candidate is so weak, I think I can still win the general election by running as an independent." Crampton flashed a playful smile.

There was a pause. Now Hawkins knew how Crampton felt when he first visited *him*.

"You're not worried that we'll split the vote and elect the Republican?"

"No. I think if I'm in the general election, I'll get a lot of Republican votes, and I think if I can pull enough of those votes while holding on to thirty-five or forty per cent of the Democrats that voted for me in the primary, I've got a good chance of beating both of you."

"That's one way of looking at it."

"It's that or retirement." He leaned in and for the first time since they'd met, Crampton seemed incredibly intense, serious and earnest. "And I do *not* want to retire."

"Why don't you move over to K Street and join one of those law firms and be a lobbyist? You'd be a valuable asset."

"I don't want to be a lobbyist. Such scumbags. They've got a stranglehold over the Congress as it is."

"Well, then you'll just have to run against me—and lose," Matt smiled as they touched glasses again.

"It was a nice thing you did when you came around to tell me you were gonna run against me. I'm here to repay that courtesy," said Crampton.

"Thanks. I appreciate it."

They parted as friends, and Hawkins went on to beat Crampton *and* the Republican in the election, bringing in fifty-three per cent of the vote.

No runoff.

Chapter 20
At Sea in *Fearless*

Executive Officer Lieutenant Rafael St. Clair took the slip of paper from a seaman who'd just come from the radio shack and held it under the light suspended over the darkened front rail of the bridge on the U.S. Coast Guard Cutter *Fearless*.

At the same time, Captain Billings made his way onto the bridge from the port side door and came over to stand beside St. Clair.

"Anything interesting, mister?"

"Message through DRMC Sector Key West from the park rangers at Fort Jefferson, sir. Seems they've had a raft land there with a half dozen Cubans aboard."

"And they want us to repatriate them, right?"

"Yes, sir."

"Rafters?"

"Yes, sir."

"That'll take us a little out of our way."

"Yes, sir."

"We won't get back to Miami for another twelve hours."

St. Clair didn't say anything. He found that the less he said around Captain Billings the better. It seemed like every time he opened his mouth or expressed an opinion, the captain jumped all over him. Of course, given their awkward personal relationship, that could be no surprise. So St. Clair found it the wiser policy simply to say nothing, or to say the very least he had to without appearing to be rude or insubordinate.

Skye Billings looked at St. Clair through the indirect dim light refracting off the hard edges of the metal on the bridge. They could just see each other's outlines, though their eyes glistened in the half-light. Without looking at his watch, St. Clair guessed it to be about 0300 hours.

"No, sir, not for at least twelve hours."

Quietly, so no one else on the bridge could hear, Billings said:

"And it's Raven's birthday."

"Yes, sir."

Billings looked at him sharply.

"I don't want to miss her birthday."

"No, sir."

Billings looked away, out ahead. In a much louder voice, he said:

"Plot a course for Fort Jefferson, Lieutenant, and send a signal through DRMC Key West that we are on our way."

"Yes, sir."

"Establish direct communications with the ranger station at Fort Jefferson."

"Yes, sir."

"Also, see what other ships—Coast Guard or Navy—are in the area that might make the trip to Cuba for us. I've noticed a little problem with our rudder controls that concerns me. Got a report from Chief Renzo about this a couple of days ago."

"Aye, aye, sir."

St. Clair saluted smartly and Billings nodded, bringing his hand up casually to return the salute halfheartedly, and turned to leave the bridge.

When he was gone, St. Clair turned to Ensign Doheny.

"Ensign, plot a course to Fort Jefferson where we will pick up some Cuban rafters."

"Aye, aye, sir."

"And go to the radio shack and get me a list of any other military vessels within two hundred miles that might render assistance by repatriating the Cubans to Havana. We have a rudder problem."

"Aye, aye, sir!"

Doheny disappeared through a hatch.

There was nothing wrong with their rudder, St. Clair knew, because all the paperwork having to do with the ship went through the executive officer's hands before it went up to the captain. Chief Renzo had merely put in writing that the rudder needed to be examined within the next 90 days to meet a maintenance requirement. St. Clair knew that Billings had only mentioned this "rudder problem" out loud on the bridge so that he could send a message (to him alone) that he was using this as an excuse to get back to port in time for Raven's birthday.

As Billings had confided to him when they were on better terms, "Raven, as sexy as she is, can be a little high maintenance, know what I mean?"

And yes, Rafael St. Clair knew exactly what he meant.

Chapter 21
Kornilevski Calls

It was 7:13 A.M. when the phone rang in the Chevy Chase house of Secretary of State Thomas P. Uptigrow. Only half asleep, his wife punched him in the arm on the third ring.

"That's why it's on your side, big shot."

Uptigrow, whose already burning stomach ulcer hadn't benefited from the indecisive election results, hadn't been in bed more than two hours. He wanted to reach out and slug his wife, but he was used to her sarcasm by now, and hadn't been laid by the grumbling woman in five years. Instead, he reached a weary arm out and picked up the phone.

"Yes?"

A heavily accented operator said:

"Hold for Ambassador Kornilevski."

Uptigrow rolled his eyes. *What in God's name does the son of a bitch want at this hour?*

"Who is it?" asked his wife.

"You don't wanna know."

"I can't wait to get outta this town," she said groggily as she rolled over into a fuzzy oblivion.

And for his part, Thomas P. Uptigrow couldn't wait, either. He'd been a happy undersecretary of state for Latin American affairs when Norwalk tapped him to replace his original secretary after he'd got himself embroiled with a time-share scandal in the South Pacific. It didn't take much to ruin a career in Washington these days, he mused. But the strain and pressure of the "promotion" had been too much for his ulcers, too much for his wife, and now this career diplomat couldn't wait for Norwalk's term to expire so he could take early retirement and move back home to Kansas City.

"Mr. Secretary?" came the urgently hushed voice of Fyodor Z. Kornilevski, a voice Uptigrow knew intimately.

"Yes, Mr. Ambassador, this is he. Can't this wait? I don't know any more about the election than you do, and—"

"It's not that, Mr. Secretary, it's just that I must insist that we meet. It's of the utmost importance."

"Meet? Now? What about?"

"I cannot discuss the subject on the telephone." There was a beat. "I, uh, I'm sorry to wake you up."

"It's not like I was really asleep," Uptigrow said testily, the sound of his overweight wife's snoring now rising as she slipped into a deep slumber. Uptigrow envied her almost irrationally.

"And how is Mrs. Uptigrow?"

"She's doing better than I am right now."

"It would be preferable if you came to my embassy for the meeting."

"When exactly did you want to meet?"

"Within the hour."

A heavy groan.

"And it can't wait, absolutely can't wait?"

"No, and I cannot discuss the delicate matter over the telephone."

"You said that already. I'll see you in an hour," he rang off, thinking, *This better be worth it, you motherfucker!*

Chapter 22
The Kremlin Dilemma

In Moscow hours earlier, when the ramifications of the stalemate in the Electoral College were beginning to be understood by Russian analysts, a hurried meeting took place between the President of Russia and Foreign Minister Nikolay Mikhailovich Lebedyev. The President paced back and forth in front of a huge fire burning in a fireplace Lebedyev thought must be at least eleven or twelve feet high. A man of normal height could not reach the mantelpiece, which was decorated with various gifts the President had received over the years from foreign dignitaries.

Lebedyev and several aides sat in chairs facing the President's desk as their leader droned on about the "delicacy" of the "situation." Lebedyev could tell the man was scared shitless. Suddenly, the President stopped.

"Did you hear me?"

Lebedyev snapped out of his reverie. He'd been focusing his attention on the stuffed head of a huge antlered deer, one of several mounted above the massive fireplace, obviously moldy relics from Czarist days. The President was not known for killing animals, just people who disagreed with him.

"Yes, of course, sir."

"Then do you agree?"

"There is risk associated with either choice, Mr. President."

"Spoken like a true *dip-lo-mat*," the President spat. "Well, I've made up my mind—we will issue the ultimatum to the Americans. You, Lebedyev, will deliver this message directly to Norwalk, and you'll do it personally."

"Very good, Mr. President."

The President came over and took Lebedyev's hand, pulling him up out of his chair and close, almost a hug.

"I can see it in your eyes, Nikolay Mikhailovich. You think I'm being too rash."

"Only you can make the decision, sir. I can only advise."

"But you advise bluffing, give them the deadline and then not act on it."

"That is my advice."

"No, I reject it! We will attack!"

"Yes, Mr. President."

"You and your people go. The plane is waiting."

His mission was quite simple, really, Lebedyev thought as he and his staff were taken by helicopter to the private Blededov Airport where they were to board a Skorsk-class X-2 aircraft—the fastest they had—for the flight to Washington.

Lebedyev was to inform President Norwalk that Russia would unilaterally attack China twenty-four hours after Lebedyev delivered his message.

They were couching the attack as *defensive* in nature, timed to prevent China from diverting water from the Black Irtysh River through the newly built Mao Canal where it would join the Karamai River. Air strikes would concentrate on the earthworks built to channel the water away from Russia.

The attack would come from the Mongolian frontier in the north (to draw a million Chinese soldiers away from the area of concern) and the Xinjiang in the west, a direct route to the canal operations.

Most important, Lebedyev was to emphasize Russia would not, repeat, *would not*, use nuclear weapons of any kind, even tactical. Such restraint (and the use of conventional arms) was meant to show the invasion was defensive in nature, given the provocative nature of the Chinese leader's anti-Russian posturing.

Lebedyev's mission was to enlist Norwalk's neutrality. The Russians already knew Norwalk favored their position. They thought it better to get on with their attack policy while the White House still housed a President who was on their side, rather than wait to see who would get elected to replace him.

The Chinese weren't waiting to finish the Mao Canal completely. The Russians couldn't afford to wait, either.

It was hoped that by sending Lebedyev on this trip at the eleventh hour, the Russians could persuade Norwalk to join them, at least emotionally, since he'd made it very clear to the American people that he thought China was acting as the aggressor and that Russia was the aggrieved party. Norwalk had a lot of credibility in Europe and elsewhere.

Lebedyev did not agree with his superior, however. Lebedyev thought he was wasting his time—one long trip to Washington for a few hours, leg cramps and discomfort all the way, a few meetings with the insufferable Kornilevski with his sweaty forehead and nervous bluster. A twenty-minute meeting with Norwalk.

And then the long trip back. More leg cramps.

No, *he* thought the best they could hope for was Norwalk's silence on the issue. He was after all what the Americans called a "lame-duck" President, and he didn't think Norwalk would find it prudent to side too publicly with the Russians. The best they could hope for from Norwalk, Lebedyev thought, was a studied neutrality, a pointed silence. Norwalk had to pretend to leave the matter of American policy with the incoming President, whoever that might be.

Lebedyev ordered a double Strindof vodka from the steward as the plane taxied down for takeoff, tossed it back and then ordered another one.

"Chill it a little more, will you?" He glanced at an aide across the aisle. "Even in this plane," he said, admiring the excellence of the craft he was in, "it's a long journey to Washington."

Chapter 23
Carrera Marble

A little before 9 A.M., the elevator doors opened onto the wide marble-floored foyer of the penthouse at Miami Tower (formerly the iconic CenTrust Tower) and Ramona Fuentes walked out into her little fiefdom.

She never failed to think of her husband Héctor the very minute the doors slid open, even before she raised her eyes to see the name of the law firm stenciled on the high glass doors that led into the reception area.

The sight of the marble immediately took her back to the quarry in the little town of Carrara in northern Italy where Héctor had "dragged her kicking and screaming," as he would later tell their daughters with a huge laugh.

"Can't we just go to Hialeah and choose the marble from the samples?" she had asked. He had looked at her with that look he sometimes got when he knew it was impossible to explain to her why he was right and she was wrong. He just shook his head slightly and muttered something under his breath.

But drag her he did to Carrera on their very next trip to Europe.

"Why don't you go on," she had said that morning when they were having a delicious room service breakfast at the Villa Medici in Florence. "You

148

choose the marble. You have the best taste in the world, Héctor, and Raven and I'll catch up on a little shopping." She had put the words in such a casual way that for a minute she thought he might go along with her, but he started shaking his head again, and he had that smile: that smile that made her fall in love with him when she was so very young.

"No," he said firmly. "You will come with me and so will Raven. I will teach you both a lesson today."

So off they went in a hired car for the short drive (about sixty miles) northwest of Florence. The town lay along the Carrione River at the base of the Apuan Alps. Up they went as far as they could go by car until they had to get out and walk.

There they went into the quarries and together— the three of them—they chose the marble that would later adorn their law offices in Miami. Some of it was white and some of it was a bluish-gray.

"Porque aqui, papi?" asked Raven.

"You ask why here, Raven? I will show you 'why here'."

When they got back to Florence through a driving rainstorm, Héctor told the driver in perfect Italian (he had studied with a tutor after they got rich and made many trips to Italy thereafter) to take them to the Galleria dell'Accademia. They got out in the pouring rain in front of a not very imposing four-story building built in the 1500s and went in.

There was an eerie calm in the place. Héctor led them down a long corridor until they found themselves in the circular room called the Tribuna where they feasted upon the giant statue of *David* by Michelangelo.

They were silent for a long time until Héctor said, "Whenever you walk into our new office, you'll think of this moment and remember that you're walking on the same marble that made this masterpiece."

And Héctor—as always—was right. Only she and Raven had those feelings—the other two girls hadn't been along.

"¿Café con leche, Señora?" Lourdes said for the second time.

"Uh, si," said Ramona. "Si, si, por favor."

She had walked through into reception, not hearing the usual greetings from her colleagues and on down the long hallway to her corner office before coming out of her flashback.

"Mr. Gilbertson asked to see you the minute you came in," said Lourdes.

"Derek can wait until I've had my coffee."

"Si, Señora," said Lourdes, moving into the outer office.

Ramona swung around in her big leather chair and looked out over the expansive view of the Port of Miami and the inlet called Government Cut that the big ships used to get to the open ocean.

Her head was still ringing from last night—she'd had way too much to drink with Sofia and the girls at the Raleigh when they were celebrating not losing to Thurston. How Lourdes got in on time was beyond her.

Lourdes came back with the blessed coffee and Ramona immediately ordered another one. She was just beginning the second cup when Derek Gilbertson came barging into her reception area and made a beeline to her office before Lourdes could do anything but shrug to Ramona through the glass wall that separated the two rooms. Ramona nodded back to Lourdes that it didn't matter, he was here now.

"Good morning, Derek," she said as pleasantly as she could manage.

"Sorry I couldn't make the Raleigh last night."

"You missed a hell of a party, Derek."

"Well, he didn't win," Derek said with a twisted frown.

The glass is always half empty with Derek, she thought. She wondered who he'd been sleeping with last night.

"He didn't *lose*, either," she pointed out.

"Well, that's true."

"What's on your mind?"

"It's about those papers for Dade International Bank."

"DIB. That would be Howard Rothman, right?"

"Yes, Howard wants us to expedite them so he can get on with that series of transactions."

"I've sent them down to financial to be vetted. As soon as I get them back, I'll sign off on them."

Derek made that little sigh people do when they're impatient.

"Whatever you say, Ramona."

"Yes, Derek, it *is* whatever I say. I just buried Héctor four weeks ago, so it's going to take me a little time to get up to speed, OK? You know I don't do financial analysis very well. I have to rely on other people's input. So I'd appreciate it if you'd cut me a little slack and not be such a spoiled turd."

"Sure, I'm sorry. I didn't mean to be insensitive."

Looking at this handsome blond stud, she could clearly see what Raven had found so attractive in him. Though she and Héctor begged her not to marry him, Raven wouldn't listen. She was as stubborn as her father in many ways. And she'd nagged them and nagged them until they agreed to bring him into the family firm, one of the top three in Miami.

"Don't worry, mi querida," Héctor had said back then. "I can handle the blond Nazi, Ramona, I can handle him."

Ramona had gone on to take a prestigious Federal judgeship, appointed by President Bush. She had to resign to come back to take over the firm after Héctor died suddenly.

Of course, by that time, Raven and Derek had been divorced for a couple of years.

So now she was stuck with Derek, stuck with the law firm and there was no Héctor to guide her.

Derek had begged her to let him take charge of the firm, told her that the last thing she should do was give up her position on the Federal bench, an achievement that had made her so incredibly proud once she had attained it.

But there was something Héctor had said on his deathbed, something about Derek.

"What is it, amorcito?" she remembered asking. "Tell me what it is."

"I want you to be careful," Héctor had said, his breath labored as he struggled to live a few more minutes. "There's something I have to tell you about DIB."

"Dade International Bank?"

"Si. DIB. Something going on with DIB, down in Quito or Tegucigalpa."

"In Ecuador? What?"

"Derek, the Nazi, he's been pushing—"

"Derek?"

"It's something I've been meaning to tell you about, but—"

He clutched his chest and Ramona had made him settle back to rest. But he died before ever telling her what he was looking into, what he suspected Derek was up to down south.

"What do you want me to tell Rothman?" asked Derek, bringing her back to the present. He was still prodding her.

Lourdes came in.

"Your nine-thirty is here, Señora."

"All right. Send them in."

"Did you want to keep the reservation at Le Zoo for lunch with your daughter?"

Ramona caught a glance of Derek's eyebrow shoot up.

"Which daughter is it, if I may ask?"

"My daughter your ex-wife, Derek, if you must know. On the DIB matter, I'll get you an answer in a couple of days. Lourdes, confirm the reservation, get me another café con leche and also get me Barry in financial."

Chapter 24
The Gilded Cage

At 9:15 A.M., Patricia Vaughan luxuriated in her bath. The hot water felt so good in the chill of the room.

Horizon, the old house where she lived on Prospect Road, was built in the 1910s, and as grand as it was, it was always a little drafty in the winter.

Of course, she was alone in the house except for the servants, her husband Jonathan preferring his Park Avenue penthouse to the house in Washington. As she relaxed in the warm, sudsy water, she marveled at how she could be estranged from Jonathan and still only be thirty years old. Though she spent quite a good deal of time thinking about her and Jonathan, she still hadn't figured it out.

He was the one with the socialite heritage. *He* was the scion of a family with a railroad fortune whose founder had been a vicious rival of Cornelius Vanderbilt. *He* was the one with all the money. *He* was the one who could have married anybody he wanted.

But he chose her, swept her off her feet with his dazzling good looks, whirlwind courtship, the stuff of fairy tales. She was the daughter of a successful New York lawyer, had lived in Georgetown, working at the U.S. Mint, and met Jonathan at an office party on N Street.

All right, she admitted, the sex had been a bit perfunctory: even more, downright dull, but she allowed herself to be swept up in all the high society, the money, the parties, all the goodies that went with the territory. She got along beautifully with Jonathan's mother, Bedelia, the grande dame of the family who lived on a nearby estate, Castledome. What more could she have wanted? She was determined to work on the quality of their sexual relationship once they settled into married life, but it didn't quite work out that way. She never had a chance.

About a month after the honeymoon, the intermittent sex died off completely, Jonathan started spending more time at their New York residence, and finally she forced a confrontation with him and he admitted he had a boyfriend in New York: Rolando, a young diplomat with the U.N. legation from El Salvador.

"Where the hell's El Salvador?" she remembered screaming at him.

He said he loved her, nothing would change in her life, she'd have everything she needed, nothing to worry about.

"I simply won't be in your life anymore," he said nonchalantly, except on those rare social occasions when he had to make an appearance in Washington.

Then he'd walked out, saying he'd be staying at a suite at the Willard when he was in town with Rolando. When in town without Rolando, he said he'd stay with her at Horizon, "if it's all right with you."

Hell, it was *his* house.

It was all so matter-of-fact that she didn't feel *anything* the first few days. No tears, no screaming matches, no throwing of priceless vases or valuable china heirlooms. In fact, the first thing she did when she collected herself was to go to the musty library on the other side of the house where she found an atlas and looked for El Salvador. She wasn't even sure if it was in Central or South America. Not that it mattered.

Once, when Jonathan was in town without Rolando and staying overnight at Horizon, she'd made a catty comment.

"Rolando's from El Salvador?"

"Yes," Jonathan had said, interested for a moment that *she* was interested.

"I looked it up. It's a *small* country."

He wasn't having any of it and quickly put her in her place.

"Well, that would be the only thing about Rolando that's small," he'd said, and walked out to the garden.

Then, months later, she woke up one day, was being served a light breakfast in the morning room, and realized quite simply that she was all alone. She was thirty years old and all alone. Yes, both her parents were alive, and her brother and her sister.

But she was all alone. In the very way that no woman wants to be.

Though she cared nothing for politics, she still lived in Washington, and the town was all about politics whether she liked it or not. The lover she'd taken, about two months after Jonathan set off the bomb exploding their marriage into smithereens, was a politician—Neil Scott, a congressman from Montana. Nice guy. Patricia had the feeling that what

Neil most enjoyed about their affair was he was cheating on his wife, and not getting caught. The "danger" of it all. Patricia thought the whole thing was a mess—and a bore—and she meant to end it all after the Inauguration in January, when Congress came back to town for the new session.

At the moment, though, she was deep in thought about the inconclusive election. She'd had a call early that morning from Bedelia, not known as an early riser, and Bedelia was all atwitter about the election.

"It's not the election, dear," Bedelia had said, "it's about your annual Thanksgiving party."

The fact was, all of Washington's top hostesses were out of town for the holidays and would be making—as of this morning—feverish plans to return to Washington to open their houses. But Patricia Vaughan's Thanksgiving party was in a mere two weeks.

"I hadn't really thought about that," Patricia had said to Bedelia.

"Why, dear, your party will be the most important social event prior to the Congress returning to name a new President. They'll crawl over each other to be there."

Bedelia said she would come over in a couple of hours to help Patricia revise and expand the invitation list.

As she drifted away in thought, Patricia was certain she didn't want to turn into Bedelia Vaughan, hooked on this or that power broker, playing the game of politics and society. Yes, Bedelia had made a life of it, but Patricia wanted something more.

It had never occurred to her when she first met Jonathan and he introduced her into this new world that her fairy tale would have a real fairy in it.

Chapter 25
Beer and Coffee

Omer Flores arrived in Miami and left the plane with the flow of other passengers, walking what seemed like a mile to get to the main terminal building.

He scanned the crowd waiting for arrivals after he cleared customs, saw nothing (and no one) unusual, slipped into the nearest bar that was just opening and ordered a cold El Presidente and a café con leche and watched as his fellow passengers were greeted by friends, family and business associates.

Again, he saw nothing unusual.

After another beer and another coffee, he got up, grabbed his lightweight duffle and moved down to Concourse E where there was a bank of lockers. He opened one and took out a cell phone, powered it up and called Derek Gilbertson.

"Hey, it's Omer."

"You just getting in?" asked a groggy Derek.

"Yeah, delays and things. Wanna meet?"

"Can't right now."

"So, what's up?"

"I'm pushing things through as fast as I can without drawing too much attention. Héctor dying has slowed things down. I'll explain when we meet."

"And when's that gonna be?"

Derek paused.

"I'll call you later and set a time."
He hung up abruptly.
Omer Flores didn't like people hanging up on him.

Chapter 26
From Russia with Love

In Washington, Thomas Uptigrow rubbed his aching stomach, swallowed a pill and chased it with a glass of water as he fidgeted in the back of the limo taking him to the Russian Embassy.

He'd had to wake up three or four of his staff, order a car, alert his security detail—all the usual hassles involved in moving about in Washington these days. Of course, when queried why he wanted to go to the Russian Embassy, he had no answer because the son of a bitch Kornilevski wouldn't tell him. Once his wife needed a carton of milk for a cake she was baking. Could he just go out and drive to the nearest little market? Of course not. The taxpayers laid out several hundred dollars for that half-gallon of milk as five or six security agents got involved in getting it back to the house. Kansas City never looked so good.

The limo, led and followed by armored Suburbans carrying his security detail, slid unobtrusively onto a ramp leading to an underground garage below the Russian Embassy. In a few minutes, he was sitting in Kornilevski's office, watching the big bear of a Russian diplomat pace nervously back and forth behind his desk.

Uptigrow had always thought Kornilevski was the most unlikely diplomat he'd ever met. The poor man was so *nervous*. Uptigrow's mother would've called him a worrywart.

"If you'll tell me the problem, Mr. Ambassador, perhaps we can move on."

"I need for you to arrange a meeting with President Norwalk," said the flustered ambassador, wiping his brow with a sopping handkerchief. An aide was serving coffee, a strong brew the rich and satisfying aroma of which almost made Uptigrow swoon. He loved coffee, and the smell of this coffee was heavenly, but he knew what it would do to his stomach. Kornilevski couldn't even wait for the aide to bring the coffee to him, but went over to the sideboard and picked up a cup as soon as it was poured.

"A cup for the secretary," Kornilevski snapped.

Uptigrow had to do it.

"A lot of cream," he said with a mischievous wink. He made a note not to tell his wife about the coffee later when he was doubled over in pain.

Uptigrow took a cautious sip of the steaming brew. A rare smile crept across his careworn face: the smile of satisfaction.

"And when exactly did you want to meet with the President, Mr. Ambassador? You know he's up to his neck with the election, and he has to address the nation today at one."

"I need for him to meet with us at eleven A.M., before he makes his speech."

"With *us?*" Uptigrow raised an eyebrow.

Kornilevski explained that Lebedyev was already in the air, due to arrive in Washington within two hours for a top-secret meeting with Norwalk.

"But what's he coming here *for?*" Uptigrow asked.

"Well, I'm, uh, I'm not, at liberty, uh …"

Uptigrow looked at the pathetic Russian Bigfoot.

"Didn't they even tell you?"

"It's of the *utmost* importance, Mr. Secretary. That's all I'm allowed to say."

Which meant, of course, that they hadn't even told their own ambassador what the secret journey was all about.

Uptigrow signaled the aide standing by the sideboard.

"Let me have another cup of that coffee, will you?" The aide rushed over to get Uptigrow's cup. "It's so much better than the Folger's crap they'll give me when I get to the White House."

Chapter 27
Four Heads

Harold Loughton, Ambassador Lord Ellsworth of Great Britain, placed his tea cup in the saucer and winced at the Royal Crown Derby design: Red Aves, it was called. He wasn't exactly sure what "aves" meant, but the English bone china was most certainly *red!* There just seemed to be too many birds cluttering up the design. They looked like large pheasants or some such fowl with long tails, somehow elegantly dangerous creatures—one of them even had a predatory look, rather like that bird in the painting pulling out the bloody heart of a most reluctant Prometheus. Was it Titian? Or Tiepolo? Or Rubens? They all used a lot of red, those Renaissance painters. One could not be entirely sure.

Lord Ellsworth was still pondering whether to ask someone about Prometheus and Titian when the first secretary buzzed him.

"It's the German ambassador, my Lord."

"Right. Show him in. You come along as well."

In a minute, Franz Meitner and Ellsworth's first secretary were sitting across the desk from him and a servant finished serving them tea.

"I'll have another cup, as well," he said. "Then leave us."

"Yes, my Lord."

The servant poured a dash of milk into Ellsworth's teacup as Ellsworth noticed Meitner looking at the Red Aves design. He would have to get it replaced. This was definitely a gift from some little old English lady who'd moved to America and wanted to give a gift to the embassy.

"Herr Meitner, I suggested this meeting for obvious reasons."

"What do we do—what *can* we do—about the election?"

"One could as easily ask what *should* we do?"

"Yes," Meitner said in a low voice. "But we agree that we ought to try to do *something*, yes?"

"I think so, yes. You and I have long been in agreement that we must do whatever we can to influence the Americans to support the Russian position over the Chinese."

"But our governments both demand neutrality."

"Yes, but now, with the election …"

"Undecided …"

"I believe, Herr Meitner, that we should take the initiative and do what we can—behind the scenes—to influence the outcome of the election in Governor St. Clair's favor."

"And our governments?"

"We would have to move in secret, without telling them. That's why I called you here today. We have no time to lose."

"Ah," the German ambassador hesitated. Meitner was not what one thought of when one thought of a *German* ambassador—he was not the tall, blond, heel-clicking count one associated with members of the German diplomatic corps, but a short fellow with a bad complexion and curly black hair. And, curiously enough, nervous.

"If you agree with me that it's *essential* the Americans continue to support the Russian line …"

"And I do agree."

"Then you'll agree we should at least explore our options?"

"Yes, of course, explore our options."

"Good," Ellsworth said, rising with a nod to the first secretary. "Show in the others."

"Others?" Meitner looked alarmed.

"I've taken the liberty of inviting the Japanese and French ambassadors to join us—I'm sure four heads will be better than one."

Chapter 28
The Candidates React

A little later that morning, a big meeting was wrapping up in Thurston's campaign headquarters. Running mate Governor Dexter White of Nebraska had flown in, Niles Overton from Minnesota, all the important players on the Democratic side.

"If we could come up with some way to ensure electors vote the way they're supposed to vote, throw this thing into the House, why, we oughta be able to nail it," Overton said, summing up everyone's thinking.

"Well, if either side gets an elector to change their vote, it'll all end up in court," said Epstein.

"And neither side wants that," Thurston added.

"Not with the timetable—we've got to have an inauguration in January," White said.

"And we want to avoid the courts—remember the Bush-Gore fiasco?"

"And the current Court is full of Republican appointees."

"The best thing," Thurston said, "is to wait till Norwalk makes his speech, analyze it, and come up with our game plan then."

Mumbling all around as everyone agreed.

Niles came over to Thurston.

"I'll be locked up in a room a couple of floors down with my people vetting the members."

"Good."

"I'll know in a couple of days who's on our side a hundred percent and who we have to worry about."

"Okay."

"Then we'll mount a charm offensive, Mr. Candidate," Overton smiled, "and let you do what you do best."

"You mean wring their necks if they don't come over?"

"Hey, it's what you're good at—a velvet glove and a heart of nails."

Niles Overton went away with his aides, leaving Thurston momentarily alone to look out the window into the grimy city below.

Overton was right. Overton with his clear-rimmed eyeglasses and bulging eyes, hair receding too early, big ears. Obviously the last guy chosen for pick-up basketball games—if he'd ever even played one. No, he was always in the library poring over books, kind of the way he would be for the next two days cloistered with his staff and living off room service food till he had his final list of who needed to be "dealt with."

That's where the charming, good-looking, athletic candidate would come into the picture. Shake their hands, but don't let go, looking them in the eye face to face while the grip got ever-so-slightly tighter, getting them close enough to smell your cologne, the most intimate moment they'd ever had with a man— that was his secret. Mental intimidation that carried with it an almost physical threat. Very few could resist Frederick Thurston's full-court press. Old timers said he was better at it than Lyndon Johnson. (And a helluva lot better looking.)

* * *

The mood was quite a bit more somber at St. Clair's headquarters. The Republicans had rented two entire low-rise buildings in Bay Harbor Islands just north of St. Clair Island and just west of Bal Harbour.

St. Clair and his closest advisors were huddled in a crammed conference room.

"I can't guarantee anything if this moves to the House," Duncan Olcott was saying. "The Democrats have us beat."

"But there's still eight split delegations," Senator Degraff added. The Vice Presidential candidate had flown in from Tulsa an hour ago.

"That's where we have to make up the difference," St. Clair said.

"Dunc already has a team working on the lists," said Lewis Ames, the campaign manager.

"Yeah," said Jack, "we'll know by tomorrow morning where everybody stands. A lot of it will have to do not just with party affiliation but with where the members stand on the China–Russia issue."

"It sure looks like Norwalk has painted us into a corner," St. Clair said in a soft voice, not at all like the big roaring voice they were used to hearing.

Jack shook his head and winked at his dad.

"That man's up to something, Governor. It's not like him to throw in the towel."

"No, not like him at all," St. Clair agreed.

"Jeffrey Norwalk is no fool."

"No, he's no fool," St. Clair agreed with Jack again, twice in the same day.

Chapter 29
Joint Base Andrews

One of the good things about Joint Base Andrews was that a plane could land secretly with no press to record the fact and no prying eyes.

Uptigrow's people at State had set everything up, so when Lebedyev touched down at Andrews, he was there to greet him with Kornilevski. But before meeting with Kornilevski to go out to Andrews, when Uptigrow had been at the White House waiting for Norwalk to come down to talk about the meeting with Lebedyev, Uptigrow had gone down the hall to spend a few minutes with Norwalk's national security advisor. Just to "catch up" on any new intel on the Sino-Russian situation.

He'd been told only that there was great tension along both the Xinjiang and the Mongolian borders, that both sides were bolstering their reserves.

Back at Andrews, both Uptigrow and Kornilevski left the VIP lounge when told Lebedyev's plane had landed and the debarking airstairs ramp was wheeling up now. They hunched their shoulders against the stiff wind and the now more rapidly falling snow and made their way to the base of the airstairs as Lebedyev led the way down followed by his retinue.

"Welcome to Washington, Minister," Uptigrow said, shaking hands.

"Very good to see you again, Mr. Secretary," Lebedyev said wearily. "A long flight."

"Yes, I know."

Kornilevski held out his arm to an SUV, but Uptigrow raised his hand.

"Since this is not a formal visit and we're not standing on ceremony here, I thought it best if you come with me in my car and we'll talk on the way to your embassy."

Once he had them in his car and they moved out of the base in a nondescript motorcade, Uptigrow got down to business.

"Can you tell me what this is all about?"

"I'm sorry, Mr. Secretary, but my instructions are to deliver my message directly to the President. I would hope that you'd be present, of course."

"You know the President is extremely busy with, uh, with the election."

"Of course. It is the indecisiveness of the election that necessitates my trip."

"I went over some new intel when I was in the White House this morning. Our satellite reconnaissance shows quite a bit of activity along your borders."

Lebedyev raised his eyebrows.

"Which side?"

"Both, I'm afraid, but more on yours, both in the north and in the west."

"Will I be able to meet with the President before his speech?"

"No, there isn't time. I'll drop you at your embassy. You'll have a few minutes to freshen up, and then we'll send a team to bring you to the President immediately after his speech."

"But the message I bring from my President should be heard *before* President Norwalk makes his speech."

"The President's address will concern the election only. That's why he scheduled you after his speech."

"But …"

Uptigrow shrugged indifferently.

"The President likes making speeches. If what you have to say is important enough, he can always make another one."

* * *

Inside his office at the Chinese Embassy, Ambassador Yang Kuo-ting and his staff were busy trading hectic messages with Beijing. The back and forth flow had been going on ever since the election stalemate.

The foreign minister in Beijing kept asking for more intelligence on President Norwalk's "policy," and how it was likely to change between now and January when the new Congress convened, but as far as Yang Kuo-ting could tell, Norwalk's pro-Russian policy hadn't changed in eight years. Why it would suddenly change now, he couldn't imagine. But of course this is not what he cabled back to Beijing. They never wanted to hear the truth. They wanted to hear what they wanted to hear. So he told them he was "working on it."

All he was working on this minute, though, was a cup of hot tea.

His government was just days away from making the Mao Canal operational. For several weeks past, they'd reduced the flow of the Black Irtysh and kept the water confined to a huge reservoir—the largest in the world—almost daring the Russians to bomb it again. Now there was so much water bottled up in the reservoir that the Russians were fearful of what kind of calamity would result if the water was released all at once if the dams were bombed.

Soon the water would flow gently and steadily into the Mao Canal and over to the Karamai, effectively devastating Russian agriculture for generations to come.

But for all this to come to pass, Beijing needed *time.* Time, time and more time.

Beijing wanted Yang Kuo-ting to buy them this time.

By holding off the Americans from tilting one way or the other *while Norwalk was still in power*.

By the time a new President was installed in January, the powers in Beijing thought the balance would shift in their direction.

If they could make that happen, they were confident the Americans would not intervene. To stand between Russia and China in such a conflict would be suicide.

Chapter 30
The Speech

Eric Stathis, Norwalk's chief of staff, made his way into the elevator for the short ride up to the living quarters of the White House.

He got out and went to the central hall where Norwalk was sitting by the large fan-shaped window at the far end making last minute changes to his speech. There'd been no speechwriters involved.

"It's time, Mr. President."

"All right, Eric."

Norwalk took a sip from the glass of iced tea on the table next to him, collected his papers and followed Stathis to the elevator.

"You sure you don't want the boys to go over your speech, Mr. President? They're waiting if you want them."

"I know what I want to say, Eric. One good thing about being a lame duck is you can quack all you want and they can't do a good God damn about it."

Stathis muffled a chuckle.

"That's right, Mr. President."

"So what are your career plans after all the grandeur and low pay you've experienced serving your country?"

"I guess I'll end up lobbying for one of the big agribusiness concerns I've been talking to."

"Make a bundle with those boys."

"Yes, sir. My retirement fund has been a little depleted in my years serving the country. My income plummeted, but my wife's bills at Neiman Marcus didn't. Not that it hasn't been an honor."

"Well, it's make up time, then."

"Yes, sir."

What else could they do, really? When a President moves into office, he brings as many of the best minds with him as he can, and they take extraordinary pay cuts for the "honor" of serving their country. Of course, everyone knows (everyone but the voters) that they'll make up for the lean years big time when they go into lobbying or business after their years in government. His whole executive staff had been feathering their nests the last eighteen months of his administration, making plans to parachute out of office and into cushy jobs where the big money awaited them, and Eric Stathis would follow all the others—like ants—over to the deep pockets smelling of a rich, lush green in K Street where the lobbyists hung their hats and swung their dicks.

As for him, well, retired Presidents usually got paid handsome fees for making short speeches and giving good "Photo Op" to the assholes who hired them for such gigs. They'd send a private jet to bring a retired President to speak for fifteen minutes and then spend an hour or two taking photos with him. Reagan got a couple of million for one trip to Japan. Clinton had made untold millions after he left office. At least he was loquacious. The idiot George Bush (the son) made millions as well, though not as much as Clinton.

It was he, Norwalk, who had brought the Republican Party back from the mess it was left in by Bush, Cheney and the other arrogant neocons who had commandeered the party for their right wing agenda.

Norwalk had tried to raise salaries—dramatically raise salaries—to make government service more palatable, hoping that he could, if not stop, at least minimize what he called the Rape of the Treasury by special interests working with ex-government officials. But even his own people regarded such a move with horror. They knew if they just bided their time, they'd make out just fine down the road. The special interests would pay them for their access to government, and the out of the loop taxpayers would, as always, pay for it all.

"So, Eric, are you going to call me Jeff Norwalk after I'm not President anymore?"

"No, Mr. President."

Norwalk laughed, then glanced at the papers he was holding.

He knew what he wanted to say, all right.

There were only two important items in his speech.

The first requested all governors in states not already legally compelling electors to vote for their slate to call special sessions of their legislatures *immediately* to pass laws within one week to force electors to vote properly. The stated motive was to ensure the will of the voters was not violated. His unstated motive was to make sure the current tie in the Electoral College *remained* that way, automatically sending the election to the House. In the House, he would have a little more wiggle room. No surprises from some anonymous elector from North Dakota who wanted to be a star. No, the four walls of the House chamber would be just enough working room for Norwalk's agenda to play out.

The second item called a special session of the lame-duck Congress to convene immediately, ostensibly to pass a resolution supporting the states in requiring electors to vote properly. The unstated motive was to get all current and future congressmen to Washington right away so Slanetti could go to work on them without any delay. There wasn't much time between this Wednesday in November and Inauguration Day in January. A lot had to happen, and it had to happen *fast*.

Chapter 31
Camp David

"And I assure the American people—and our allies and adversaries around the world—that the American democracy that has been the fiercely burning light on the hill for over two hundred years is strong and solid. We *will* elect a new President according to the dictates of the Constitution. There *will* be a smooth transition. And there *will* be no interruption in the grand tradition of peaceful transfer of power from one administration to another. I give you my word, under God."

There was a round of applause from the staffers gathered in the Oval Office as he finished his speech.

Eric Stathis made sure everyone cleared out fast enough and then made his way over to Norwalk.

"They're already up at Camp David," he whispered.

"Good. Let's go."

Norwalk and Stathis moved immediately out through the French doors and onto the South Lawn on their way to Marine One. They were airborne in a couple of minutes. Some of the senior staff looking after them were puzzled. Norwalk usually traveled with a larger retinue, even when he went to Camp David.

Settled aboard the chopper, Norwalk thought it was a stroke of good planning to set the meeting up at

Camp David. No wagging tongues would see them there.

He looked down at the horse farms around Frederick, Maryland, over which they passed on their seventy-mile trip. Up ahead, he saw the Appalachian Trail atop a ridge in the Catoctin Mountains near the site of Camp David. His second year in office, he told the Secret Service to get a detail together and some camping gear, and they went to the Trail and hiked all the way to Harper's Ferry. Took two days. The brilliance of the stars at night is what he most remembered—and the steepness of those god-awful inclines.

Marine One touched down and Norwalk stepped off followed by Stathis. They went immediately to the Oak Lodge in the middle of the camp where Uptigrow would be waiting with Kornilevski and Lebedyev.

"What in God's name do you think this is all about?"

"Beats the hell out of me," said Stathis.

"To travel all this way so secretly."

"Doesn't look good."

"No," said Norwalk as they went through a door snapped open by a Secret Service agent waiting on the porch.

There were the usual warm greetings and salutations. Norwalk and Stathis were offered coffee by the Navy steward on hand.

"You know, it's after two o'clock," said Norwalk, "and I've already had a rough day. Bring me a Johnny Walker Black on the rocks."

Lebedyev and Kornilevski exchanged glances, put down their coffee and asked for vodka.

"Just a little more milk," Uptigrow asked the steward when he got around to the secretary of state's coffee.

Once they'd all taken generous gulps of their respective libations, Norwalk sent the stewards out, leaving the Americans and the Russians alone with their translators. But both Russians spoke in English.

"Mr. President, I regret the extreme secrecy of my trip, but my President thought it necessary given the circumstances."

"And what 'circumstances' would he be referring to?"

"Our intelligence has learned the Chinese are on the verge of opening the locks to the Mao Canal. To make the damned thing operational."

"When you say 'on the verge,'…"

"We mean by hours or days, not weeks."

"And?"

"We are convinced the current leaders in Beijing are mad enough to provoke us."

"I cannot say I disagree with you. They are unstable, all the men at the top. Very dangerous." There was a pause. Norwalk looked sharply at the foreign minister. "And, *have* they provoked you to that point?"

Lebedyev swallowed hard and got on with it.

"We need to know this: will you condone a preventive attack to destroy this Mao Canal?"

"A 'preventive attack'?"

"Yes, in a way, it's no different from your own invasion of Iraq some years ago. You called that a preventive attack, a *defensive* measure."

Norwalk blushed. How many times had he been forced to listen to similar arguments?

"Well, that's not what *I* called it, not at the time. But I wasn't President then."

"We are gravely concerned about the Chinese."

"I know you are. So am I. But I do not think, considering I will be out of office in a matter of weeks, that I can launch so bold a foreign policy initiative on my own, leaving it to the next President to deal with. I can't do that."

"Then my instructions are to inform you that Russian land and air forces will launch a two-front *defensive* assault against China in exactly twenty-four hours."

Norwalk paused, measuring his words.

"Can I have your assurances that Russia has no long term interests in occupying the Chinese homeland?"

Lebedyev spread his arms and smiled.

"We can barely feed our own people. Who wants billions of Chinese mouths to feed?"

"I was thinking more of their coal," Norwalk lifted an eyebrow.

Norwalk had one of the translators bring him the bottle of Johnny Walker. He filled his glass.

"Fill the foreign minister's glass with vodka, will you?"

"Thank you," said Lebedyev.

"And the ambassador's as well."

"Thank you," said Kornilevski, wiping the sweat on his upper lip with the cuff of his jacket.

"Let's go for a walk, Nikolay Mikhailovich," Norwalk said as he got out of his comfortable chair by the fire, taking his glass with him.

The two of them drifted outside and started walking down a path in the woods. A light snow fell.

"It's important we prove to you our intentions. I cannot lie to you about our timing. We are most concerned about the Chinese pushing this Mao Canal to completion. Obviously they mean to finish it. Why build it in the first place? And now there's talk of another canal to divert waters from the Amur River. This is a river, Mr. President, that flows for a thousand miles once it passes from China into Russia. A loss of even twenty-five percent of its water would be even more disastrous than the loss we're facing with the Black Irtysh. And now we have your recent election to think about. We *do not* want to see Senator Thurston become the next President."

"That makes two of us."

"If Thurston does become President, we feel we will have at least made our move in time to prove our good intentions, that we have no claims on China other than our refusal to allow the diversion of so much water that has flowed unimpeded for thousands of years into Russia."

"I understand," Norwalk said, taking a sip of the burning whisky.

"We will use only conventional weapons in our attack. We will even use our advance troops as decoys. If the Chinese launch a nuclear weapon, it will prove to you our motives. And maybe then

America will join Russia to rid the world of the Chinese menace."

"All right. I can live with that. As far as the American people know, we never had this meeting. You surprise me in twenty-four hours so I can pretend to be shocked."

Lebedyev nodded. It was the best he could hope for. Maybe the long trip was worth it, after all, leg cramps or not.

They turned back toward Oak Lodge.

"We will be sorry to see you leave office."

"I'll be sorry to leave—with so many things left to do."

"Amazing, with all your resources," Lebedyev allowed himself a little laugh as he shook his head.

"What do you mean?"

"In Russia, you would not have to leave office. And if you wanted to leave office, retire to a huge villa on the Crimea overlooking the Black Sea, with money and servants, there would be no question that Governor St. Clair would succeed you."

"Really?"

"Yes, in Russia those of us in power have ways to make sure we *stay* in power."

Norwalk drank the last of his whisky, clapped Lebedyev on the shoulder and smiled.

"Well, we have ways here, too, Nikolay Mikhailovich. It's just they're a little different, that's all. But they work." He shook the ice in his glass. "Let's have another drink before you leave for Moscow."

Chapter 32
Fort Jefferson

On the bridge of the USCGC *Fearless*, Lieutenant Rafael St. Clair peered through his high-powered Bushnell S-type 4B series binoculars into the early morning gloom and saw the dark specter of Fort Jefferson appear on the horizon. St. Clair looked at his watch: 0512 hours.

The old fort, built in the 1840s and '50s in the Dry Tortugas and once known as the largest brick structure in the Western Hemisphere, had been abandoned by the Navy almost as soon as it was finished, having become obsolete in that short time. Now part of the National Park Service, the crumbling fort was an offbeat tourist attraction for day-trippers from Key West who came out on ferries and by seaplane to snorkel and scuba dive out on the reefs.

St. Clair knew that Fort Jefferson had been used as a prison by the Union forces in the Civil War. It was a remote place where most of the inmates were private soldiers who'd deserted. The most famous prisoner had been Dr. Samuel Mudd, who'd had the misfortune to set a splint on the broken leg of John Wilkes Booth, not knowing that Booth had the night before assassinated President Lincoln at Ford's Theatre.

St. Clair had to admit that, whatever it had been, Fort Jefferson made an impressive sight as its six-sided façade rose from the water. The sheer weight of all that masonry looked like it would sink the flat little island (called Garden Key) it stood on. The fort had been built around the entire perimeter of the island so that there was almost no land that wasn't enclosed within the dark weather-beaten walls. St. Clair guessed that the engineers decided on the six-sided structure because it roughly followed the contours of the existing landmass.

"Come left to course five-six-one," he said to the helmsman.

"Port to course five-six-one, aye, sir," came the automatic reply.

"Should I wake the captain, sir?" asked Ensign Doheny, stepping forward.

"I don't think so, Ensign. Let's let the captain rest. We'll call him when we pass the reef."

"Aye, aye, sir," Doheny said, stepping back.

It would be just fine with Rafael St. Clair if they never called Captain Billings at all. This man was a thorn in Rafael's side like no other.

It was bad enough that Billings had a chip on his shoulder because he'd worked his way up through the ranks, unlike Rafael, who had attended the Coast Guard Academy in New London, Connecticut. There was often this sort of perceived friction between Academy graduates and "the others." Rafael did all he could to discourage any sense of "difference" between the two types of officers, but the tension was there nonetheless, especially strong among those who hadn't attended the Academy.

But that wasn't half of it, not with Skye Billings.

Rafael had to deal with the fact that his dad was the Governor, and to dispel any suggestion that he might be getting preferential treatment. With such a famous and powerful father, Rafael had been very scrupulous to avoid any idea of getting a break here and there along the way in his career. He actually thought he was treated worse because of his position.

But the biggest pain in his ass involved his captain's continuing affair with Raven Fuentes, his brother Jack's ex-girlfriend.

Skye and Raven had gotten together not long after Rafael came aboard *Fearless* as the new executive officer. There had been the usual tension between a captain and a newly installed first officer that was to be expected, but when a couple of months into his new post Billings mentioned he was seeing Raven Fuentes, Rafael's first reaction had been to laugh and say, "You *are* kidding, right?"

No, he hadn't been kidding at all.

The dark cloud that had passed over Billings's face that morning hadn't gone away in over a year, and in that year he'd done everything in his power to make Rafael's life fucking miserable.

Then, of course, Jack couldn't seem to get the Fuentes family out of his system after throwing over Raven, making Raven hell-bent on revenge. No, he had to start sleeping with her younger sister Babylon, further complicating things.

Fearless approached the main docks at Fort Jefferson and tied off. St. Clair observed all this from the port side of the bridge. Captain Billings came up behind him.

"Everything in order, Lieutenant?" he asked, glancing at a slip of paper in his hand.

"Yes, sir."

"Go ashore and see to the transfer. We got lucky. USS *Runnymeade* is making for San Juan from Miami and they will take our rafters back to Havana for us. We'll meet them at sea, transfer the rafters and make way for Miami from there."

"Very good news, sir."

Billings didn't like the lifelessness in St. Clair's tone or the emotionless way he spoke whenever they talked, but there wasn't much he could do about it.

"Go ashore, then, see to everything."

"Yes, sir."

St. Clair went down the gangway with some guardsmen and was greeted by a park ranger.

"Lieutenant St. Clair," he said as they shook hands.

"Chief Ranger Al Gonzalez, Lieutenant. Welcome to Fort Jefferson."

"Thanks. I've been here many times. One of my first diving trips was out here. My dad brought me and my brother in a seaplane."

"Yeah, you're the Governor's son, Rafael St. Clair, that's right!"

St. Clair shrugged and smiled.

"I confess. I am."

Gonzales started pumping his hand all over again, this time with an excited smile.

"Well, I want you to tell your dad that I voted for him. Everybody stationed here voted for him."

"I'll tell him that. Now, about the rafters …"

"Yeah, I've sent word to bring them out."

Gonzalez turned around and St. Clair followed his gaze to a half dozen Cubans shuffling out to the dock, guarded by park rangers carrying rifles.

"If these guys landed here, they'd be covered by the 'wet foot, dry foot' policy. Why are they being repatriated?" The U.S. policy dictated that if Cuban refugees' feet touched dry land, they could come into the U.S., but if they were interdicted at sea, they would be immediately repatriated.

"One of our patrol boats caught 'em a half a mile out at sea."

"So they're 'wet feet,' then."

"Yeah."

"But there're not all rafters. One of them's a fisherman. We picked him up after his ship sank."

"Oh?"

As the rafters walked by them, Rafael thought one of them gave him a searching look. More than that. A *beseeching* look. An imploring look that told Rafael he had something to share with him but was afraid to spill the beans in front of everyone. *That* kind of look.

"How do you even know these guys are Cuban?"

"I talked to a couple of them. They're Cuban. I'm Cuban myself."

"Yeah, me too," said Rafael.

"Funny thing, though," said Gonzalez.

"What?"

Gonzalez turned toward the other end of the dock and started walking. Rafael followed him. At the end, Gonzalez pointed down to a sparkling new Zodiac tied off at both ends. Next to it was a pathetic crumpled raft heavily beaten up by its time in the sea.

"The rafters came in that. The 'fisherman' came in that Zodiac."

"Nice Zodiac."

"Poor Cuban fishermen don't have boats like that on their ships."

Gonzalez pointed again to the Zodiac. But this was no simple inflatable boat. It was constructed more along the lines of a Combat Rubber Raiding Craft, or CRRC. This was one expensive Zodiac. From what Rafael could see, this inflatable might have been made to the strict specifications required by the SEALs or the USCG. (They had a similar boat aboard *Fearless*.) The engine looked like a 55 horsepower two-stroke engine with a pumpjet propulsor. This had a "shrouded impeller," designed to reduce the risk of any injury to people in the water around it, so it was much less dangerous than an open prop.

Rafael looked back over his shoulder as the "rafters" were led up the gangway into *Fearless*. The man who'd looked at him before looked over his shoulder once more. He had that same imploring look. Something that said, *Help me!* This made Rafael determined to have a word with him once they cast off to rendezvous with *Runnymeade*.

"It does look odd," Rafael said to Gonzalez.

"Yeah."

"Which one is the fisherman?"

"The one looking at us right now."

"What'd he tell you?"

"That his ship sank and the other crew members went down with it. He just had time to get aboard the Zodiac. But then the engine died and he was adrift until we picked him up. But I went in and tried the engine."

"Yeah?"

"Worked perfectly," said Gonzalez with a snide smirk.

"So he's no fisherman."

"No way he's a fishermen. And another thing?"

"Yeah?"

"There was blood in the Zodiac. Mixed in with the seawater, there was blood. I know what blood smells like, you know?"

"Yeah. Find any weapons?"

Gonzalez extended his arm over the wide ocean vista.

"Plenty of places to hide weapons out here." He paused and looked at St. Clair. "Plenty o' places to hide *anything,* when you think about it."

"So you think he might've killed the crew? Some kind of drug thing, you think?"

"Could be," Gonzalez shrugged. "But then, could be anything. He's not saying, though."

"Huh," said Rafael. "Well, we see everything out here, you know?"

"Said he'd been adrift for two days. But I looked into the kit where the food and water are stored. Pristine condition. He never took a sip of water and never ate anything. For two whole days adrift at sea?"

"Yeah," said St. Clair with a reaffirming nod.

"That's for sure. And another thing about him."

"What?"

"Fishermen—they have a smell, a certain kind of smell, you know?"

"Yeah."

"He didn't have it."

St. Clair nodded.

"I better get going."

"Sure."

"Nice to meet you. And tell your dad we're right behind him through all this election deadlock bullshit."

"I will. Thanks."

St. Clair shook hands with Gonzalez and walked briskly back to *Fearless*.

Chapter 33
Coffee at Enriqueta's

Omer Flores pulled into the tiny parking lot of Enriqueta's on the corner of Second Avenue and 29th Street in Wynwood. He didn't see Derek Gilbertson's car. He parked and went up to the open window to order a colada and a café con leche.

He got the Styrofoam cups of steaming coffee and went to stand under a clump of palm trees to sip his colada. He was halfway through when he saw Gilbertson park on the other side of the street and come over to him.

"Hey, Omer," said Gilbertson.

"Hi, Derek," said Omer, handing Gilbertson the café con leche. Gilbertson immediately pulled the plastic lid off and took a gulp.

"Nothing like Enriqueta's, you know?"

"Yeah," Omer smiled.

"Good Cuban slop," said Gilbertson.

"I like it." Omer didn't like people who put down Cuban food.

"Best steak sandwich in town, though" said Gilbertson, getting the message.

"Yeah, I know. We've had enough of them, right?"

"Yeah."

"You've been through the mill traveling."

"Yeah, but it's over."

"For a while," said Omer.

"For a while, yeah."

"What's the update on the shipment."

"I couldn't talk on the phone," said Gilbertson.

"I understand," said Omer.

A breeze came up and they both took sips from their cups.

"We got the last twenty million wired out through the usual shell companies."

"Including KLX?"

"Yeah, about three mil to KLX."

Flores nodded. The edge of his lips even twisted up slightly to form what Gilbertson thought might even be a smile. Omer Flores was not easily given over to the concept of smiling.

"That's nice," was all he said.

Gilbertson could see Flores doing the math in his head. The most recent $500,000 deposited to KLX Corp. would bring its holdings to some $8 million. And there were only four partners lined up to split this money.

"We got lucky on another front."

"Yeah?"

"I sent another ten million back in a empty sub after Sinaloa unloaded down in the Keys."

"Hey, that's great. Gives us a break from the wire transfers."

"That's what I thought. They were going back with God knows how much of their own money and had plenty of room, so I only had to pay a $250,000 carriage fee."

"Who do we have on the other end?"

"My guy Mario at the other end. But we got extra lucky. Larry Duarte is with the sub's crew."

"That's too lucky to be true."

"But it is."

"Larry got word to me about the drop in the Keys, and I was able to broker the deal through their people here after Mario made the connection and this way we get the ten mil out through the sub."

"Very nice," said Flores.

"That gives us maybe two mil of the ten that we share, and it's not in the KLX accounts."

"The usual four ways, right?" Flores said with a little jump in his right eyebrow.

Gilbertson knew this was Flores's way of questioning whether their fourth partner working on the inside at KLX was to share the extra $2 million, or if Gilbertson planned on cutting out the fourth guy and splitting it between him and Larry Duarte.

Gilbertson pursed his lips, and tried to put on an expression that indicated he was mildly offended.

"No, Omer. It's for all four of us."

"Well, sure. It ought to be."

"Well, of course."

The breeze had died and now Gilbertson felt uncomfortable in his suit, a prickly sweat forming under his arms.

"When can we start drawing out of KLX?"

"Soon. Soon enough."

"It's been a while."

Gilbertson agreed that it had been a while since they got into business together. But everything had gone well so far, and he didn't want to make any suspicious moves till everybody involved was in the clear and disappeared below the radar.

"I just want to wait till Duarte gets out of DEA before we start moving the money out to us."

"I'm out in about six months."

"We'll meet with Duarte when he gets back from this assignment and see where he stands."

"OK."

The breeze picked up again, refreshing them both, the sound of the wind rustling through the dry palm fronds high overhead. Gilbertson felt the sweat on his forehead begin to cool. He wiped it away with the napkin that came with the coffee, but he had spilled a little on it, and felt the sticky, sugary coffee on his forehead.

"Crazy about the election, huh?" said Gilbertson, anxious to change the subject.

"Yeah, it's going to be a mess in Washington."

"Think it'll affect us in any way?" Gilbertson wondered.

"Doubt it. The last thing any President has any control over is DEA."

"Or much of anything else, really."

"Yeah. So many layers of people."

"With their own agendas," said Gilbertson.

Now Omer Flores really did laugh.

"What's so funny?" asked Gilbertson.

"Nothing. What you just said about people with their own agendas."

"Yeah?"

"People like us."

Now Gilbertson laughed as well.

In his car across the street, Sean Walsh took a few photos of the two men standing under the palm trees, put through the plate number on Flores's car, and made the usual notations PIs made when they surveilled somebody.

He was really pissed off because he could smell the coffee wafting out from the exhaust fans atop Enriquetta's roof. And he wanted a cup, bad.

Chapter 34
Loose Ends

Later, in a black SUV taking them to Joint Base Andrews, part of an all-black six-car motorcade, Lebedyev and Kornilevski rehashed the meeting.

"It's the best we can do, then," said Kornilevski.

"Yes, but this business will not be over tomorrow, even with the invasion. Thank God Norwalk is President while we launch the invasion. We still have to deal with Thurston if he is elected."

"Yes."

"Ambassador, have you put out the word among your associates, your, uh, contacts, how willing we would be to help ensure St. Clair's election?"

"I have been making discreet inquiries."

"Good. Make them faster. We must do everything in our power to help St. Clair, and we must get this Thurston out of the way. Ah, here we are."

* * *

The reaction to Norwalk's speech at Thurston's headquarters was nothing short of jubilant. Thurston and Epstein watched as the staff, psyched after the speech, started packing for the move to Washington.

"I don't get it, Jess. It's like he's setting us up to win," said Thurston.

"Well," said Epstein, "what else could he do?"

"I don't know. It's not Norwalk."

"It's the fairest thing—make the electors vote the way they were elected to vote and let the House decide the contest according to the Constitution."

"Still …"

"Doesn't get any simpler than that," said Epstein.

"I'm sorry, Jess, but this is Jeffrey Norwalk we're dealing with here."

"I know, but we might as well celebrate good news, don't you think?"

"Yeah, but, we'll see—nothing's in the bag yet."

* * *

In Miami, the opposite mood had taken hold of St. Clair's staff. A heavy malaise fell over the office as the staff started breaking down computer stations, packing up files, preparing for the move to St. Clair's Washington headquarters. Everybody from St. Clair on down tried to put a good face on what surely looked like bad news. St. Clair made the rounds, poking his head into every office and cubicle, doing what he could to elevate spirits.

But as his own spirits flagged, he retreated to his private office and enjoyed a moment alone before Jack came in.

"What the hell do you think that was all about?" asked Jack.

"Hell if I know, Jack," said St. Clair, rubbing his chin.

"Have you talked to Norwalk? Before the speech, I mean? Did he give you any indication what he was up to?"

"Nothing."

"And nobody on his team?"

"Nothing from anybody."

"So everything in the speech was news to you?"

"Yes. Everything."

St. Clair wasn't sure what he expected Norwalk to do to improve his chances, but by sending the election willy-nilly to the House, it seemed to St. Clair that his chances of prevailing were rapidly diminishing. A call came through from Duncan Olcott.

"Hey, Dunc. What do you think of that speech?"

They talked for a minute about the speech.

"Don't worry, Sam," Olcott finally said. "We've got a shot in the House. I only say that because it's the only shot we have, good or bad. I'm not really calling about the speech. I'm calling about the list."

"Ah, yes, the list Norwalk wants. You got it ready?"

"Tomorrow we'll have it."

"OK, as soon as you have it. The President seems very interested in getting this list—the way you and your people see things—as soon as possible."

St. Clair hung up and looked at Jack, who shrugged.

"Maybe Norwalk has something up his sleeve."

"He'd better have something up there. We're gonna need it, Jack."

"I know."

"Look, I really appreciate all the time you've taken away from running the island and the agency and everything else—just to help your old man."

"Rafael would be here doing the same thing if he wasn't on duty so much, you know that."

"Well, seeing as how we don't get along politically."

"Hey, Dad, it's the biggest joke on the campaign trail. A Republican candidate with a Democratic son."

"I just wanted to, uh, *say it*, you know?"

"Thanks, Dad. Whatever happens, I love you, don't forget that."

"I won't."

The buzzer sounded.

"Yes?"

"Babylon Fuentes is here for your son, Governor."

A smile came over the old man's face.

"Send her in."

"Ah, Babe!" said Jack.

St. Clair shook his head.

"You and these Fuentes women, for Christ's sake."

"This one was an accident," Jack protested.

"That whole family is an accident," St. Clair said with a laugh.

The darkly delicious Babe Fuentes came in and gave Jack a big hug.

"Hello, Jack," she said before going around the desk to give St. Clair a kiss on the cheek. "And you, Governor, how are you holding up? This whole thing must be a nightmare for you."

"It is."

"And Sofia? How is she?"

"Fine, a little tired like the rest of us, but she'll be all right."

"Give her my best, will you?"

"I will."

"You ready, Jack?"

"Yep."

"Where are you two headed?"

"I'm dropping Babe to meet her mother and sisters for lunch at Le Zoo. I've got to pick up a watch being repaired—the Rolex you gave me—and then I'm going home to finish packing with Gargrave."

"Are you bringing Gargrave up to Washington with you?"

"He'll be covering for me on the island, but he'll come up if we need him for anything."

"Good man you have there in Gargrave."

"Don't tell that to Babe."

"He's always creeping around," she said with a shudder. "I don't like it."

"He lives in the house same as I do, Babe. Get used to it." He took her in his arms and kissed her.

"All right. I'll get used to it."

"See ya later, Dad."

"Go on, you two. I've got some packing to do myself."

As the door closed behind them and he sank back into his deep leather chair, he remembered what Jack had said about Norwalk having something up his sleeve. If the old man had a trick or two remaining before he left the Oval Office forever, this was certainly the time to spring them.

He shook his head to try to clear away the cobwebs. He wouldn't know any more until he got that list Olcott was working up into Norwalk's hands.

* * *

Babe stopped to talk to someone she knew on the campaign staff at the same time Jack got a call from Gargrave. He walked a couple of feet away and took it.

"What's up, Gargrave?"

"Just to let you know you're all packed for Washington, sir."

"I'll be coming back and forth, you know?"

"Yes, sir. Everything will be fine while you're gone, sir."

"Anything that needs attention?"

"Nothing. Walsh is on surveillance of Derek Gilbertson as you ordered. Might have something interesting for you."

"I see. Good."

Jack wondered what mischief Derek Gilbertson was up to.

"I'll go over pending cases at the agency with you, but otherwise, everything's in order," said Gargrave.

"See you shortly, then."

"Very good, sir."

He hung up and waited for Babe to finish her little chat.

Chapter 35
Ladies Who Lunch

Ramona Fuentes pulled up to the valet station in the Bal Harbour Shops and emerged from her midnight blue Mercedes CL-Class coupé in front of all the people having lunch at Le Zoo and Carpaccio. People's heads turned.

Some of the regulars at both restaurants knew who she was. Those who didn't knew she was Somebody because of her car, the way the valet smiled and bowed politely from the neck, her manner of dress and most of all, the way she carried herself. This was a formidable woman to be reckoned with.

As she walked around her car and felt the eyes staring at her, Ramona thought the designers of this open-air shopping mecca knew what they were doing when they placed the valet station directly in front of the two biggest restaurants: there would always be hundreds of people to gawk at the well-heeled clientele as they poured out of their Rollses, their Bentleys, their Maseratis, their Lamborghinis. To be acknowledged by the valet as a regular was "something." She wondered if that's why so many of her rich friends kept coming back here.

Just recently, Christian Louboutin had decamped for the rather tacky Design District. Developers were making a Big Push to draw the top tenants from Bal

Harbour into the Design District, to give the sad-sack area a little class, but with the Design District's huge number of colorless, bland buildings and hardly head-turning architecture—nothing more than a collection of former furniture showrooms and low-level warehouses with scarcely a tree on the sidewalks, Ramona didn't think they'd ever really compete with Bal Harbour with its lusher than lush landscaping and its gorgeous fountains gushing tons of water. The fountains, she had noticed, were strategically placed so that just as the sound of the pulsating water from one fountain faded away, the sound of the next one began to rise. You couldn't go anywhere in Bal Harbour without hearing the exquisite sound of rushing water.

She and the girls alternated between Carpaccio and Le Zoo when they had their monthly luncheon meetings. As the girls got older and went out on their own, Ramona had decided that these meetings were essential if they were to maintain a tightly knit family unit.

She was even more convinced of this necessity after the sudden death of her beloved Héctor.

She approached the maître d' at Le Zoo. He greeted her warmly and took her to a table for four in the middle of the outside terrace. She wasn't there a minute before Antonia, her youngest, appeared, bright and peppy. She came over and gave Ramona a kiss and sat down next to her. Ramona didn't have to know her daughter as well as she did to tell she was madly excited about something. She felt certain that "something" was a man.

"Oh, Mother! You'll never guess who asked me out."

"A good reason not to try," Ramona said in a low voice, smiling.

The waiter came over.

"Badoit to drink right now, and a Rioja, the Marques de Riscal, later."

"Mais oui, Madame."

"You give up?"

"A long time ago," said Ramona, touching a knife to Le Zoo's creamy butter and spreading it delicately on a piece of warm crusty bread.

The humor was lost on Antonia, who leaned in and whispered.

"Rafael St. Clair!"

Ramona rolled her eyes and put her buttered bread down.

"Are you insane, Antonia?"

Antonia sat up and straightened her back, a sign Ramona knew well: she was getting defensive.

"Just because Raven had an affair with Jack doesn't mean it won't work out better for me and Rafael. He's such a dreamboat."

The waiter returned and poured the Badoit sparkling water and opened the Rioja, leaving it on the table.

"He is very handsome, that Rafael," said Ramona, making a second attempt to eat the bread.

"And he's Cuban, Rafael. Jack's not."

"Rafael St. Clair is half Cuban," Ramona corrected.

"And you get along with Sofia."

"Of course I get along with Sofia. I've known Sofia my whole life. And Jack, for that matter."

"And Sam. You and Sam are old friends."

"Yes, Sam and I are old friends."

How old and how close she'd been with Sam was not something she cared to share with Antonia—or her other two daughters, either. The only one left who knew anything about her and Sam was Sofia—and she wasn't talking. But Ramona had the feeling Sofia felt the same way about the Fuentes family as Ramona felt about the St. Clairs. Though the families hadn't actually married into each other (though they had come close with Raven and Jack), it still seemed to Ramona that they were irrevocably joined at the hip. She was sure Sofia felt the same way. Question now was: how would all the intertwined relationships play out in the years ahead. And, considering how smart all the players were, how could you ever be sure what the other players were plotting. Was anyone pulling strings behind the scenes?

The fireworks were major league when Raven and Jack broke up—or, as Ramona liked to think, when Raven drove Jack away with her insane needs and jealous rantings—but things got even worse when she abruptly married Derek Gilbertson. She'd worked on Héctor to allow him to join the firm. Later, when she divorced Derek, she created even more bad blood in the family.

"I don't even blame Jack for breaking up with Raven. I blame her."

"She's so totally jealous. Poor Jack couldn't even glance at another woman without her climbing a tree and throwing coconuts down at everybody."

Antonia giggled at the very image of her sister, clad head-to-toe in Chanel, throwing coconuts from the top of a palm tree. Apparently, the image struck a chord with Ramona as well, because she giggled, too.

"But don't you think we've had enough of the St. Clair family for a while."

"Well, now that Babe is seeing Jack, I know it's a little complicated."

"Yes, it is a little complicated."

"But you know how I've always felt about Rafael."

Ramona smiled.

How could she not know how Antonia felt about Rafael? How could anyone not know? Every time the handsome man showed up in his Coast Guard whites, his shining black hair slicked back over his beautiful head, Antonia practically melted. A blind man could see it.

Which meant that Raven saw it, too, and the very idea that Antonia would ever get close to Rafael drove Raven absolutely mad with jealousy. Meaningless, misdirected jealousy. There was something—what was the word—yes, *bitterness*, that consumed Raven that Ramona never saw in her other children. Ramona herself didn't have a deep sense of bitterness. Héctor surely never had it. Wherever she got it, she had it in spades.

Just then, looking over Antonia's shoulder, Ramona saw Jack Houston St. Clair escorting Babe past the maître d'. Babe had never looked more beautiful or fulfilled, which would make any mother happy.

"Let's not mention that you're going to see Rafael, all right?"

"All right, but it'll get out eventually."

"In this town, I'm sure it will. But not today, OK?"

"OK."

"Hello, Antonia," said Jack as Babe went over to give Ramona a kiss. Jack followed and kissed Ramona. "Ramona, you're looking as lovely as ever."

"You're an idle flatterer, Jack. Just keep it up."

Everybody laughed.

Jack tossed a furtive glance at the empty chair as he went around to kiss Antonia on the cheek.

"Antonia, how's everything?"

"Just great, Jack. It's really something about the election, huh?"

"Yeah, I'm running around crazy, getting ready to move up to Washington to help dad through this whole mess."

"What did Sam think of the speech?"

"He's confused by it. Seems like Norwalk is throwing Dad into the lions' den by forcing the issue into the House."

"What else could he do?"

"That's what we're asking ourselves."

"Maybe he has a plan."

"Somebody better have a plan," laughed Jack.

"I've got some business up in Washington next week, Jack," said Ramona. "Where are you staying?"

"Dad's got a big suite at the Willard, so I'll be there with him." Jack looked fine in a pair of khaki slacks, a light blue pin-striped shirt and a fitted Navy blue blazer with dark blue bone buttons.

"Maybe we'll squeeze in a lunch if you and your dad have time. Though I doubt he'll have any time, not with all he's got to go through."

"Definitely give me a call."

"That's right. It's only, like, ten weeks to the inauguration, correct?" said Antonia.

"Yes," mused Ramona. "A lot of arm-twisting to be done between now and then."

"I'm going to go up for a few days, too," said Babe," tossing her lustrous black hair over her shoulder. "This is all so exciting."

She wiggled in her chair like a child, which of course to her mother she was and always would be. Ramona may have been middle aged, but that didn't mean she was beyond appreciating a fine specimen of the male body when she saw one. There was no question the qualities in Jack that had attracted first Raven and now Babylon. He was an ex-SEAL; having left the Navy under mysterious circumstances that nobody really knew anything about. And he had that thick but lean body shared by most of the men in Special Ops. His hands were large and rough looking, like a carpenter's, but when you touched them, they were smooth and gentle. He had a firm hard backside, broad shoulders that tapered down to a narrow waist and a flat stomach. The first (and last) word that you thought of when you thought of Jack Houston St. Clair was "masculine."

"Gotta run—a million things to do, you know?" said Jack with a quick wave and a broad smile, leaning down to kiss Babe on the cheek and turning to leave.

"Yes, go. Don't let us keep you. Our best to Sam," said Ramona.

"Thanks. I'll pass that along."

They all watched him go.

And they all watched him run into Raven Fuentes as she slipped past the maître d' and almost collided with Jack. Before he bumped into her, he stepped back, the way you might when confronted with a poisonous snake you wanted to give a wide berth. They exchanged a couple of words and then Jack disappeared around the corner.

"He's got to pick up a watch they're repairing," said Babe. "I'm glad Raven didn't bite his head off."

"I'll bet," said Antonia. "You want him all to yourself."

"Wouldn't you?" Babe smiled.

"I certainly would," said Antonia, "but I have my eye on something just as nice."

Antonia winked at her mother, who raised an eyebrow in warning as she imperceptibly shook her head.

Raven came over clad in Chanel from head to toe except for the Hermès scarf folded delicately around her neck and flopped down in the chair across from her mother. The waiter appeared.

"Stoli on the rocks. Two limes." The waiter nodded.

"I'll have some wine now," said Ramona, and the waiter poured out some of the Rioja.

"Me, too," said Babe.

"I'll stick with the water for now," said Antonia.

The waiter disappeared, but not before Ramona noticed him giving Raven an admiring glance. To herself she thought, *She's a firecracker, that one, but she still has what men love.*

Raven turned to Babe, her eyebrow arched.

"So, Babylon, I see your babysitter dropped you off."

"You weren't complaining when he was babysitting you," Babe snapped back.

"Oh, Babe, you're so—"

"Girls, girls, girls," Ramona interrupted before things went too far. "We're here for *lunch*. Not a mud-wrestling match."

"Sorry," said Babe.

"Me, too," said Raven, though her tone made it quite clear she didn't mean it.

Ramona stole a look at Antonia, whose smile said, "If only these two knew about Rafael."

"I missed you at dinner the other night, Raven," said Ramona.

"Something came up at the last minute," said Raven, reaching for a piece of bread, thinking twice, returning it to the bread basket.

"You can't put bread back in the basket after you've touched it," said Antonia.

Raven shook her head and squinted her eyes at Antonia, took the bread back from the basket and put it on her bread plate where she left it untouched.

"Oh, please. I'm just *not* eating any bread."

"It's the butter here that's so good," said Ramona, buttering up another piece of bread. "We had a good time at Casa Juancho. You missed their paella, your favorite."

"I know, I know. That's my favorite restaurant. It's just that I forgot about something I had to do."

There was a pause as the others waited for Raven to continue. She looked up.

"Something I had to do," she said in a tone that indicated that was all she was going to say about it.

What she wasn't telling them was she'd gotten a call that night from Skye Billings, who *had* to see her before leaving for a sudden assignment on *Fearless*.

There had been passionate men in her life before Skye, Jack most certainly being one of them, but there was something about this man that she found totally compelling.

And this was one romance she was not going to tell her family about, especially since Skye was the reason she'd broken up with Jack.

The waiter came back with his little pad.

"I'll have the salad Niçoise," said Ramona.

"Oh, God," said Raven as she looked over the menu. "I'll have the marinated white anchovies and the steak tartare. No main course."

"I'll have the steak frites," said Babe, "medium rare. After last night with Jack I've really worked up an appetite."

Raven looked at Ramona and shook her head.

"She won't quit, this little bitch."

"Hey—" Babe started.

"Stop it, girls, stop it right now!" Ramona commanded.

"I'll have the salad Niçoise also," said Antonia, "but with a side of your fries. I just love those skinny fries they have here."

The waiter nodded and, after pouring more Rioja and Badoit, left.

"Girls, if I've told you once, I've told you a thousand times: you only have each other. I don't care who you marry, who you're sleeping with or anything else. You will always have each other, and you need to rely on each other like your lives depended on it."

"I know, Mother," said Babe, turning to Raven. "I'm sorry."

"I am, too," Raven said, leaning over to kiss her sister on the cheek.

"Do I have to be the first one to start crying?" asked Antonia, making everybody laugh.

"Oh, what the hell?" said Raven with a final laugh, snatching up her knife and spreading butter on the piece of bread she'd put aside.

"That's right, Raven, live!" said Antonia.

Raven thought how surprised Antonia would be if she knew how fully she had been living these last six or seven months since breaking up with Jack.

It wasn't something she'd planned. It all happened quite naturally, or so it seemed at the time.

The three girls had followed Ramona like the little obedient girls they were when Governor St. Clair invited them down for the ceremony installing Rafael as the new executive officer of *Fearless*. Given Ramona's close relationship with Sofia, there was no question that they'd attend. And Raven was seeing Jack at the time, so everything seemed fine.

When they went through the receiving line to meet the officers after the installation, Skye shook hands with Jack first, and then her, but the way he held her hand for those extra four or five seconds, combined with the way his blue eyes looked into hers—well, she knew she was hooked. She could feel a surge of white-hot heat flash through her body like a lightning strike.

A month later, things exploded between her and Jack.

No one knew why. And she wasn't about to tell. The truth was that she was furiously jealous of Jack, madly so, senselessly so. And, looking back, she knew it had all been in her mind. That he had loved her. And that it was her wild jealousy that had driven him away. It didn't help her ego that he was now sleeping with her younger sister.

"We haven't seen much of you around the house lately," said Antonia.

"I've been busy. I got four new clients last month alone."

"Like the one in Jamaica?" asked Babe.

"Yeah, I was there over two weeks."

Her family didn't need to know anything about the "client" in Jamaica. Even that there really was no client in Jamaica. The only person she'd visited during those two long steamy weeks in Jamaica was Skye Billings.

And she planned on keeping everything about their relationship a secret. At least until she knew where it was really going.

Chapter 36
Perryman's Call

Later in the afternoon, Norwalk was in the Oval Office with his appointments secretary.

"What's this from Lamar Perryman?"

"Yes, Mr. President. The congressman called while you were up at Camp David."

That's curious, thought Norwalk. *Wonder what the old coot wants. It had to be important—he wouldn't call otherwise.*

"I'm going up for an hour or so."

"Yes, Mr. President."

Norwalk always tried to read for an hour or two in the afternoons if his schedule permitted it, and to take a half-hour nap. He remembered reading years ago that Winston Churchill always took an afternoon nap, even during the height of the Battle of Britain.

Up in the living quarters, Norwalk opened the book he was reading, David McCullough's *John Adams*, a fine book he'd put off too long. He settled down with a whisky and had the operator get Perryman on the line.

"Lamar, how are you? Congratulations on your reelection."

"Thank you, Mr. President. I would arrange a meeting with you, but given the circumstances, I don't see how we could meet without arousing suspicions."

"Suspicions? You and I have been on good terms for years—that's no secret."

"I know, but I want you to know that Senator Thurston has decided that the caucus name me speaker while Niles Overton works behind the scenes on the members to ensure his election."

"Well, actually, that makes a lot of sense," Norwalk nodded, taking a sip of his whisky. He'd had four drinks today, but he felt like he hadn't had any.

"Not when you know that I fully support your position on the Sino-Russian situation, and that I will do everything I can to assure St. Clair wins the vote in the House."

Norwalk almost choked.

"But you've been very careful to stay out of this mess, Lamar."

"I've been keeping my own counsel because I never saw that my influence mattered. Now it counts."

"And Thurston has no idea?"

"Not a glimmer of suspicion."

"Lamar, when they make the announcement that you're the new speaker, I'll have you up to the White House for a courtesy lunch or a dinner, make it real formal, so we can get some time together without arousing their curiosity, and we'll talk. I'm gonna need you big time, Lamar."

"I know you will, Mr. President. And I know why you're calling the Congress back into session. We can't work on these people if they're scattered over fifty states, now can we?"

"No, we can't, Lamar."

"We have a lot of work to do."

"And we'll do it, Lamar, we'll do it."

"Goodbye, Mr. President."

"Wait, Lamar ..."

"Yes?"

"This *is* the best thing for the country."

"Much as I admire you, Mr. President, you know me well enough to know I wouldn't be doin' it if it *weren't.*"

Chapter 37
Earl Grey and Snow

At Horizon, Patricia Vaughan was sipping her Ashbys Earl Grey in the breakfast room and looking over *The Washington Post*.

Politics, politics, politics, she thought. *Well, what else do you expect in this town?*

The fact that she couldn't care less for politics made it that much stranger that she was a prisoner in Washington.

Well, she wasn't exactly a prisoner, and if she was, she most certainly dwelt in a gilded cage. There was no reason why she couldn't be in Palm Beach now— they had a place there. (People like Jonathan didn't have a "home" or a "house" in Rome or Paris. They had a "place.") Or she could be in New York. Not the Park Avenue penthouse with Jonathan and his disgusting boyfriend, but a suite at the Waldorf Towers, which is where Jonathan had an apartment that was hers to use.

She could be in London, or Paris, or anywhere the hell she wanted to be, but the reason she remained in Washington was—well, a malaise had settled over her. A listlessness. Lack of drive. Lack of desire. Lack of motivation. *A lack of living is what it is*, she thought suddenly, and she was even sadder than before when she realized exactly what was bothering her.

Something caught her eye and she looked up. It was snowing, just a little, but enough to get you excited.

Emily came in to clear just as Patricia took her tea bag out and put it on the bread plate.

"Emily, go get me one of your cigarettes," she said.

"But you don't smoke, Miss Patricia."

"Well, I do today."

"Yes, Miss."

Emily had a pack on her, and was just lighting the cigarette for Patricia when Simkins came in with some paperwork.

"Ahem," Simkins said by way of announcing his presence.

Emily made quick business clearing the dishes.

"Yes, Simkins?"

"You have luncheon today with Mrs. Vaughan, Madam, and I wondered if I might suggest a menu."

"Suggest away, Simkins."

"Mrs. Vaughan is particularly fond of shrimp Louis and I thought a cucumber soup to start."

"Okay with the salad, but it's too cold for cucumber soup. Let's have that southwestern chili and chicken soup I made up for her a couple of months ago—Cook has the recipe. I made it from scratch. Bedelia loved it. She likes spicy food, did you know that, Simkins? Well, you worked for her for … how many years?"

"For fifteen years, Madam. I learned of Mrs. Vaughan's extreme fondness for spiced foods when I was in her service."

"Look at the snow, Simkins. It's wonderful. Let's have lunch in here instead of the dining room. It's so nice out here when it's snowing."

"Very good, Madam," Simkins smiled a kindly smile. She knew Simkins liked her, even if she wasn't the most proper hostess in all Washington.

"By the way."

"Yes, Madam?"

"Were you called Simkins before you became a butler, or after?"

"Before I became a butler I was called Freddie, at least by my mother and by my wife."

"Maybe I should call you Freddie."

"Simkins is fine, Madam."

She reached out and took his hand.

"Thanks for being here with me, Simkins."

"It's my pleasure to serve you, Madam."

He withdrew and she turned her gaze to the yard outside, quickly turning white as the snow fell at a faster clip. She was very lucky that Bedelia had sent Simkins over to run Horizon after Jonathan decamped for New York to be with Rolando, the hated boyfriend, taking his own butler with him.

Bedelia had been great through the whole process.

"What's another scandal in *this* family?" she'd said when word got out all over town that Jonathan was queer.

Patricia loved the breakfast room when it snowed. It had glass on three sides. On the side facing the garden, the whole wall was made up of large windowpanes, from floor to ceiling. Huge French doors on either end of the little room gave out into the yard. And the ceiling also was glass, with vines running up and down. It was quite romantic.

She even liked it at night, especially in the rain. She felt like she was in a little glass box, cozy and warm, with the rain pitter-pattering down.

Her smile faded and she frowned.

Correction.

Alone in a glass box.

Chapter 38
A Chinese Monkey Wrench

The next day, well before the Russian assault, Norwalk summoned the Chinese ambassador to the White House. He had a few hours before the Russians advanced into China and he wanted to make the most of them.

Uptigrow and his undersecretaries for Asian affairs were all there when they sat down in the Oval Office with Yang Kuo-ting and his people.

"I must congratulate you on your speech, Mr. President."

"Thank you, Mr. Ambassador."

"It will be a pleasant experience for me to deal with a President who believes in the integrity of the Chinese position."

"It would be a lot easier to support your government if your government would meet the international community half-way. Many perfectly authentic proposals have been put forward to help alleviate the water issues you're now using to create friction with Russia."

"You are being very—" Yang Kuo-ting looked at his translator and said something in Chinese and then turned to Norwalk—"you are being very *blunt*, Mr. President. Blunt."

Norwalk leaned forward, smiled and put his elbows on his desk, staring the ambassador dead in the eye.

"I only have a few more weeks in office, Mr. Ambassador, so I'll say what I want to say. I would advise you to do the same. Then maybe we might get somewhere."

It went on like this, back-and-forth, back-and-forth, with Norwalk failing to gain any traction with the man. It was obvious by Kuo-ting's superior manner that he was just going through the motions with Norwalk, doing him a courtesy, waiting until January when Thurston would be inaugurated and he would have a sympathetic shoulder to lean on.

After an hour, Norwalk gave up and sent the man packing with dire warnings about the dangers of provoking Russia. Norwalk even thought he detected a sneer on the Chinaman's face as he bade him farewell.

A few minutes after Kuo-ting left the White House, as his three-car motorcade (with motorcycle escorts front and rear) turned off Pennsylvania Avenue and made its way down M Street heading toward the embassy, a Ford Taurus station wagon coming in the other direction exploded just as it passed the middle car in the motorcade, the car carrying the Chinese ambassador.

Moments later, Eric Stathis called Norwalk in the living quarters where he'd gone to read a little more of *John Adams*.

"*Oh, Christ!*" Norwalk yelled, and tossed *John Adams* aside, "I'll be down right away."

By the time he got to the Oval Office, damage reports were already coming in. Both motorcycle cops in the rear were killed, one in the front. Two Chinese security people in the front car were killed, and the four in the car behind Kuo-ting were injured but alive. In Kuo-ting's car, the driver was killed and the first secretary sitting directly behind the driver was also killed, but Kuo-ting had lived, only because he was sitting on the side of the car away from the horrific blast.

"These things are like baseball," said Stathis. "A matter of inches."

Kuo-ting was already on his way to the hospital.

"This has never happened in Washington, has it?" asked Norwalk.

Stathis shook his head.

"I don't think so. A suicide car bomb? Never."

Norwalk turned to his national security advisor and his military aides.

"How could anybody know he was coming here this afternoon?"

People shook their heads.

"And be prepared to move so quickly," said one of the military men.

"This is like Lebanon," said Uptigrow, who hadn't had a chance to leave the White House before the explosion.

"Well, you guys get started. Let's do what we have to. Big build-up at their embassy, military escorts whenever their people leave the embassy. Tighten it up. Everything."

"Yes, Mr. President."

"You know how the Chinese are, Mr. President," said Uptigrow warily. "They'll suspect we set him up."

"*Set him up?* You've got to be kidding."

"Who else knew he was coming here except for his people and our people?"

"*Fuck!*"

Chapter 39
The "Fisherman"

Back on *Fearless*, Lieutenant St. Clair waited until they had cast off from Fort Jefferson and were well under way before he tried to talk to their detainees. Or, the one detainee he wanted to talk to, the "fisherman."

They'd gone below to be checked out for any basic medical problems, given something to eat and drink and then brought back on deck for some air. They were handcuffed to a long metal rail amidships under an awning so they were able to enjoy the fresh sea air and at the same time stay out of the sun.

Armed guards stood on both the port and starboard sides watching them, but St. Clair was able to approach them with what he wanted to project was a casual interest in their well-being.

He spoke to them in Spanish, asked where they were from, how long they'd been at sea, what hardships they'd endured, what family they might have in Miami or elsewhere in the U.S.

After a few minutes of this, the guards seemed to lose all interest in following the conversation.

"Do any of you speak English? Habla Inglés."

The "fisherman" nodded.

"I do," he said softly.

St. Clair came in a little closer and lowered his voice. The rafters went back to talking among themselves and the sentries weren't listening, so it was just as if they were alone.

"You do? How well?"

"Really well."

"You looked like you were trying to get my attention back there at Fort Jefferson."

"I was."

"Something you want to tell me?" He looked at a slip of paper in his hands. "Paco Agular?"

"Yes, sir. But I didn't want to make a big scene. What I have to say is for your ears only. You and the captain, that is."

"Your English is really good."

"It ought to be. I'm American. Well, Cuban-American."

"You weren't on a fishing boat that sank, were you?"

"No."

"So, what was it?"

He looked around at the others, saw they weren't listening.

"First of all, I'm not Paco Agular, but Laurencio Duarte. And I'm a DEA undercover agent and I need to talk to you in private."

Chapter 40
"No Comment"

Norwalk, Stathis and Uptigrow squeezed into a little niche off the Oval Office where there was a TV so they could watch Senator Thurston on NBC blast the terrorist elements that attacked the Chinese ambassador when anchor Aaron Cross abruptly cut him off to report the launch of the Russian invasion in the Xinjiang and Mongolia.

Norwalk couldn't contain a giggle.

"That'll shut him up for a minute."

"Only just," said Uptigrow.

Cross turned to Thurston, who was completely flustered.

"Do you have a comment on this Russian military action, Senator?"

"Well, I, uh, I'm totally surprised. I don't know what to, uh … I think the Russians better have some kind of explanation for what's going on over there. Maybe these are maneuvers, or …"

The anchor interrupted Thurston to report on Russian air strikes deep in Chinese territory.

Norwalk's console buzzed. He walked back into the Oval Office and touched a button.

"Yes?"

"The press secretary's here, Mr. President."

"I'm sure he is. Wonder what took him so long. Send him in."

Norwalk's press secretary came running into the room, breathing hard.

"Mr. President, what am I—?"

"No comment. We have no comment."

The poor man was aghast.

"No comment?"

"No comment, that's right."

"But the whole press corps—"

"Actually, I do have a comment."

"Yes, sir."

"We're studying the situation."

"We're *studying* the situation?"

"Yes."

"But—"

"And after we study the situation, we will have—no comment."

Chapter 41
Bacon at the Betsy

Derek Gilbertson turned onto Ocean Drive and drove up to 14th Street in his Jaguar XJ and parked directly across the street from the Hotel Betsy. He laughed to himself at how easy it was to find a parking space on South Beach even in November. Yes, the town was packed, but it was also South Beach, and nobody—even the tourists—got up at 8 A.M. They were all sleeping off the debauchery of the night before.

Gilbertson got out of the car and looked at his watch. He was ten minutes early. The sound of chirping birds in the park separating Ocean Drive from the beach caught his ear and he walked through Lummus Park and out to the dune line where he saw the broad Atlantic stretch out limitlessly. The sun was already high enough to cause him to sweat under his shirt, but there was a fresh salty breeze coming in and he took a deep breath. Two freighters far out at sea passed each other as one made its way north and the other headed south to some far flung exotic destination.

He had certainly been at the right place at the right time when Raven broke up with Jack Houston St. Clair. Being in the nightclub LIV in the Fontainebleau that night and watching her go off on the poor guy was a real education. Even the DJ was so impressed with Raven's fireworks that he stopped the music completely so everybody could listen to the bitch rip Jack a new asshole. And the guy hadn't done anything.

What he did do that benefitted Derek was to leave. He just picked up and left the club, leaving her there to scream after him.

Derek picked up the ball and ended up taking Raven home that night. He'd worked his way from between her legs into the family law firm and now he was poised to make millions through his Cartel and banking connections. And the best part: she divorced him, leaving him free to play the town, including such high wire acts as Wilma Kassman.

Gilbertson looked over his shoulder and saw a couple of tourists in bathing gear and flip-flops settle into chairs on the porch of the Betsy, the sun bouncing off their sunglasses. He saw a Lexus he recognized pull up and park a couple of spots behind his car. Howard Rothman, slim and lean and smarter than most, got out and crossed the street, going into the lobby. He was setting Howard up for a very big fall, but he still had to finish building the house of cards above Howard before he could pull the trigger and have them all drop down on his head. The pieces weren't in place yet.

"Oh, Howard," he said under his breath. "What are we going to do with you?"

He walked back through the park, crossed Ocean Drive and went up into the hotel, passing the tourists as they ordered the fruit plate and "that Cuban coffee you make down here, what's it called?"

Gilbertson smiled and passed into the lobby.

"American coffee," Rothman was just telling the waiter as Gilbertson walked up. He got up and shook hands.

"I'll have café con leche, please," said Gilbertson to the sleepy-eyed waiter as he sat down. He looked over his shoulder as another pair of tourists came out of the elevator and went outside to take a table on the porch in the glaring sunlight. He and Rothman were the only customers in the lobby portion of the restaurant.

"You know, I've never been here before," said Rothman. "Heard great things about it," he added as he surveyed the immaculate lobby.

"Oh, it's great. Super steaks."

"Some Frenchman's place, yeah?"

"Yeah. BLT is what they call it. Laurent Tourondel is the guy. Try some of the pastries. They're the best—and the bacon: they don't fry it; I think they bake it or something. Best bacon in town."

"I better have the bacon then," said Rothman. "But only one or two pieces," he added, touching his flat stomach.

Rothman ordered an egg white spinach omelette, Derek the eggs Benedict.

"Raven used to love coming here."

"In better days."

"Yeah, in better days. Now I shudder when I think of her."

They got their coffee and ordered and then got down to business.

"What's the latest at the office?"

Gilbertson shrugged.

"There wasn't very much I could do after Héctor died so suddenly. Things at the firm just ground to a fucking halt."

"It was a shock all over town when he keeled over like that," said Rothman.

"And then waiting for Ramona to make up her mind about what she's going to do."

"Nobody thought she'd leave the bench to go back to the firm."

"That firm throws off millions of dollars a year, Howard, you know that. What was she making as a Federal judge?"

"Well, it's more of an honor to be a Federal judge. You don't do it for the money."

"Not if you have Héctor bringing in the cash, no. But Ramona's got those three daughters to think about, don't forget that. Antonia's not married yet. Raven and I are divorced and Raven needs a *lot* of money, I can swear to it. And Babe is sleeping with Jack Houston St. Clair."

They could smell the rich bacon even before the waiter got to the table with their orders.

"But he was an item with Raven before you," Rothman said.

"Yeah, before I married her. I think she still has a thing for Jack. It must be killing her that Babe is sleeping with him now."

There was a small pause.

"How long are we looking at before Ramona signs off on the wire transfers?" Rothman finally said.

"I'm not sure. She was going over things with a guy in our financial department. But it's all clean as a whistle."

"Till you look into it deeper."

The waiter brought fresh coffees and left them alone. Gilbertson leaned over the table.

"She won't look into it any deeper than Héctor did. If I can get this stuff by Héctor, I can get it by Ramona."

"So you think we oughta continue just the way we have been?"

"How much have you cleaned for us, Howard? You have any idea how much?"

Rothman shook his head.

"More than a couple of hundred million."

"It's closer to three hundred million, Howard. The little we shave off has made us rich just like everybody else along the pipeline. Why should we quit?"

Rothman brought both hands to his chest in a defensive gesture.

"I'm not saying we quit anything," he protested.

"All right, then," Gilbertson leaned back in his chair, picking up a piece of bacon.

"If you look at it objectively, what we're doing isn't really illegal." He caught a reproving glance from Gilbertson. "Well, technically, I mean."

"It's not illegal in Bolivia or Peru maybe, but it's illegal here." A sharp crack as Gilbertson bit into the bacon. "It's just good business, Howard. Like this bacon, it's a really good thing. Eat too much of it and you'll die of heart disease. As for our business, it's as good as the bacon. It's only bad for you if you get caught."

Chapter 42
Laurencio Duarte

Laurencio Duarte had run through his story twenty times to get it all lined up so he'd have every chance of being believed. He knew he hadn't washed all the blood out of the Zodiac. He'd been working on that when the Fort Jefferson patrol boat came up to him so fast that he ran out of time. Since he hadn't been able to wash it away, it would have to be explained away.

After he revealed his identity to St. Clair, Duarte had been left on deck still cuffed to the railing, but before long, another guardsman came up, removed his cuffs from the rail (but not from his hands) and escorted him below decks to a small spare office. Moments later, Captain Billings and St. Clair came in.

"Wait in the passageway," Billings ordered the guardsman.

"Aye, aye, sir."

When the door was closed, Billings turned to him again.

"My first officer tells me you're DEA undercover."

"Yes, sir. Name's Larry Duarte and I've been working for the Sinaloa Cartel for four years."

"So tell us how you found yourself stranded at sea."

"We were returning to Colombia in a submersible from delivering a few tons of coke to pick-up units in the Keys, took on water and were forced to abandon ship."

Billings nibbled away at his lower lip, clearly transfixed by the story.

"Lieutenant St. Clair here tells me there was blood in the Zodiac. A park ranger saw it and showed it to him."

Duarte was ready for that one.

"I'd been suspected for a while, and when we got out of the sub into the Zodiac, the crew turned on me—well, there was just one of them. The other three went down with the ship. That's how fast it went down. Well, once in the Zodiac, this guy said he thought I had sabotaged the ship because I was a spy. He attacked me. I had a small caliber weapon with me, and I shot him. But as we struggled, he got the gun away from me but I was able to push him overboard and he lost his grip on the gun and then the current took him away. That's how the blood got there."

"That's quite a story."

"Yes, sir, it was pretty scary."

"So after you push this guy overboard, you were adrift?"

"Yes, sir. The engine died on me."

"How long were you out there before the rangers at Fort Jefferson found you?"

"Two days. I had water and some food in the kit."

"Jesus. You could have ended up anywhere. You were about sixty miles from the Gulfstream—that could've taken you up to Canada."

"Yes, sir." Duarte wanted to change the subject.

"DEA section chief in Miami will verify my identity, both as Paco Agular and my real identity, Laurencio Duarte, and my status."

"We'll see to that right away. Until then, I'll have to keep you under guard."

"I understand, Captain."

Billings settled down into a chair, clearly mesmerized by all this.

"So you've been doing this for four years?"

"Yes, sir. This is my first year working in the submersibles. I've made six trips this year."

"I would *hate* being in one of those damn ships." Duarte smiled.

"I've got claustrophobia. I know what you mean."

They chatted on for a bit until Billings was called when the *Runnymeade* was in sight.

"OK, then. We'll check with DEA in Miami and get you out of those cuffs, Laurencio."

"Larry, sir."

"Larry, sure."

They called the guardsman back and left him.

Duarte felt good about the way the interview had gone. They believed him completely. And he saw no reason why they wouldn't believe the same story when he got back to Miami. Why could they imagine he would lie about it? What was there to lie about? How could they know there were 65 million reasons to lie? But, given his life the past four years, he'd become quite adept at lying.

The main point was that nobody knew about the money in *Mirta*, except the people at the Cartel tracking her, but they didn't know where *Mirta* was.

When *Mirta* failed to show up, and none of the crew later showed up proving they'd been rescued, the Cartel would chalk it up to just another lost submersible. Happened all the time. The crew members' families would all get big cash payouts to maintain loyalty—and silence. It logically would be assumed that "Paco" had gone down with the ship along with everybody else.

The Cartel would have no way of knowing he'd returned to the U.S.

Since he really was an undercover DEA agent, his story would be corroborated within the hour and the cuffs would come off.

When they tied up in Miami, he'd be picked up by a DEA team and debriefed immediately. Once he got through that, they'd give him a month off and decide where to assign him next. As far as DEA would be concerned, "Paco" would indeed have gone down with the ship. The sooner Paco was history, the better for everybody involved.

Once Billings and St. Clair were out in the passageway, Billings sent St. Clair to contact the DEA in Miami to verify Duarte's story. But as he made his way to the radio shack, things didn't add up in St. Clair's mind.

The blood in the Zodiac—even diluted as it was by seawater—seemed like an awful lot from just one man with a wound. It couldn't have been too serious a wound because the stricken man was still forceful enough to struggle with Duarte. But the story did answer Gonzalez's question about the blood.

Billings never mentioned the untouched food and water supplies. St. Clair knew he couldn't interrupt

Billings—mostly for personal reasons—so he let it pass.

Duarte said the engine died on him. Gonzalez said it worked just fine.

There was no indication of any sunburn. Duarte's face and arms were perfectly pale, consistent for a man who'd been in a submersible. Not consistent with a man baking for two days in the hot Caribbean sun.

St. Clair wondered what he ought to do about these little inconsistencies when they got back to Miami. He didn't dare speak up in any way that might make Billings look like he hadn't thoroughly done his job vetting Duarte. Better to let Duarte slip through the fingers than cause Billings any trouble.

The main thing that bothered St. Clair was why a DEA agent would lie to them about any of this in the first place? What could he possibly have to gain? Maybe he was saving certain facts to reveal to DEA when they debriefed him, thinking it wasn't any business of a couple of average Coast Guard officers. That much made sense.

Up on deck a little later, as *Fearless* made for *Runnymeade* at full speed, they passed a group of three small boats anchored together.

By now, Duarte was out of his cuffs and standing on the after deck with Billings and St. Clair.

"Know what those boats are, Larry?"

"What?"

"Part of the team that guards the *Atocha*'s wreck site."

"The *Atocha!* Hey, that's something."

The *Atocha* was short for *Nuestra Señora de Atocha* (Our Lady of Atocha), a Spanish treasure galleon that went down in a 1622 Labor Day hurricane 35 miles off Key West with millions of dollars worth of jewelry, silver and gold. Treasure hunter Mel Fisher discovered it in 1985.

Billings shook his head.

"They say they still haven't recovered a third of the treasure."

St. Clair turned to Duarte.

"Just imagine what's buried under all that water," he said with a laugh.

St. Clair found himself a little surprised when he saw Duarte's pale skin flush bright red.

"Yeah, just imagine," Duarte said in a whisper.

Bright red, thought St. Clair. *Bright red.*

Chapter 43
The Cowboy Freshman

Matt Hawkins arrived in Washington aboard Delta flight 432 direct from Cheyenne after a connection in Denver, just a couple of days after the election. But already a lot had happened: Yang Kuo-ting was in the hospital, the Russians had advanced into China and Mongolia, President Norwalk had called the old Congress into special session.

The long flight originated in the early morning. His new administrative assistant, David Murchison, and his secretary, Liz Woodbury, who'd traveled with him from Jackson to Cheyenne to catch the flight, were fast asleep. He, however, didn't close his eyes the whole trip.

He had plenty to think about. He'd heard about Yang's bombing the night before. And the Russian invasion of China a few hours later.

He continued to think about Norwalk's speech calling the current lame-duck Congress to Washington. He, too, was coming to town because the speech put beyond any doubt that the House would actually decide who the next President would be. He looked out of his window at the passing pre-dawn clouds. He hadn't thought it would happen. He'd assumed something would break in the Electoral

College or that one or two states would throw the election either way after recounts. But now, *this!* He'd be in the thick of it. A witness to history.

Matt Hawkins felt queasy. He'd never felt queasy in his entire life, never found himself in circumstances where this feeling would come about. He felt butterflies in his stomach, similar to the feeling he had when he addressed his first Rotary Club, but it was much, much more than that. He kept telling himself throughout the flight that his vote would never be that crucial. He'd been over the figures with Dave Murchison on the new Congress. His party had twenty-two states already against the Republicans' twenty. It was just a matter of the House leadership convincing one representative from a few of the states with tied delegations to join them. Knowing what little he did about power politics in Washington, he thought that wouldn't be too difficult for the House leadership.

If for some reason his vote became important later on, he knew how he'd respond. He'd supported Thurston wholeheartedly in the campaign, he believed in his China policy and though he'd never met the man, he felt a sudden closeness of spirit with the Democratic candidate. He knew his support wouldn't waver.

Also, he didn't completely trust President Norwalk. Why would a man who so obviously hated Senator Thurston (he had made that plain on earlier occasions) throw the election into a House dominated by that man's party? Hawkins didn't understand. He feared President Norwalk, but he couldn't put his finger on any actual reason. The President didn't even know who he was, so how could he fear him? The almost mystical power of "The Presidency" is what he imagined he feared.

He had to admit it: he was just a cocky mountain boy who was coming down from the hills into the real world. It was a little scary, no question about it, but scary in a *very* exciting way. *He couldn't wait to get to Washington.*

He was nervous at the prospect of entering Washington during such a crisis as the sole representative from the sovereign state of Wyoming. He felt the fear that any novice would feel, no matter what he was stepping into. He also felt the thrill rush through his blood and tingle his nerves when he thought of the challenge ahead of him. This was surely a peak higher than Grand Teton, he thought. He was strangely attracted to Washington as though to some higher goal, some idealized craggy Olympus that he felt the surging energy to race up and conquer, hard though it might be, and bruised though he might be when he got there. He felt the power that any man in his position would feel, so he knew the accompanying cold sensations of fear were not unusual. He knew he wouldn't feel the same if he'd been elected one of the twenty-nine representatives from New York or one of the fifty-three from California. A representative from New York could hardly be too important in the crisis confronting the Congress. The representative from Wyoming might be, *could be.* When he stood up on the floor of the House to cast his vote, he alone would speak for his state.

Although the President's speech was foremost on his mind, he was thinking also of Yang's bomb ing.

He wondered who did it, of course, and decided that Russian-backed commandos tried to blow up the ambassador. He wondered if the same bad guys would also shoot Thurston if they had the chance, or if they'd shoot anyone who stood for China against Russia.

Seldom had he been in a situation in which he had such a strong desire to have someone close to him. That desire came over him suddenly and he wanted Sue near him.

But Sue would remain in Jackson and Cheyenne for up to three weeks making all the arrangements that he might have seen to, had he stayed in Wyoming long enough.

He wanted to call Bill Crampton that night, if possible, and see him as soon as he could. Although he agreed election night to see Crampton before he left for Washington, neither he nor Crampton knew they'd both be leaving the next day.

He talked to the still current representative from Wyoming the day after the election immediately after hearing Norwalk's speech, and found out that Crampton was planning to fly to Washington a few hours later than Hawkins. Matt hoped they could see each other that night. He desperately wanted to hear what Crampton had to say about the situation and he still held the highest possible regard for him as a man, and his respect for Crampton's obvious practical political experience was leapfrogging by the hour, so anxiously did he feel the desire to have his counsel.

In talking to Crampton after Norwalk's speech, Crampton did not sound too sad about having lost.

"I'll bet, Mr. Congressman-elect, that you feel every single one of your twenty-nine years," he said.

Matt had to smile at that. Crampton was right.

"Yes sir, I certainly do."

"But it looks like we'll both be going to Washington. I'm leaving tomorrow at ten. When will you go?"

"We're going over to Cheyenne tonight to catch the early flight out just before dawn."

"Can't wait, huh?" said Crampton, laughing lightly. "I certainly wish I could be sitting in my old seat next January," Crampton said quite soberly. "I never thought anything like this would happen—not *really* happen. It's one thing to read about Jefferson and Burr, but this is different. It's happening to us today! Things are so different."

"How do you mean—different?" Matt asked, sensing already in Crampton's voice, the uniqueness of the situation.

"Well," Crampton said, hesitating, "*methods* are so different these days. It won't be a grand debate on constitutional forms and the integrity of one position over another. There won't be time for all that rhetoric—not with something like this. Things are much quicker now and the stakes—the stakes are so high."

"I'd like to see you when we get down."

"Of course, that's what I'd like, too. They'll probably keep the session going till after Thanksgiving."

"I don't know anybody down there—except you."

"Well, we'll talk about it more later."

"Okay, Bill, that's fine."

It was more than fine with him. Crampton's friendliness and his being in Washington meant a lot to Matt, because he literally knew no one down there. He met the Democratic National Committee chairman when the guy came to Wyoming to make a speech for him, and he met with liaisons from the national headquarters about finance and the "thrust" of his campaign, but that was all. He was in another league now.

He'd called his parents before leaving to tell them goodbye. He knew he wouldn't be back until everything was settled and a new President was named. His mother cried and said she missed him already. He was always a little annoyed with her for not admitting to herself that he was twenty-nine years old.

He thought about various things not related to his immediate position, things separated by great gaps of time: the feeling of the mountain streams rushing over his naked body when he swam in them as a youth, the girl he made love to the night before climbing Eagle Peak alone, his wedding night with Sue, his graduation from law school and his mother's perennial tears and his father's proud smile and firm handshake when he came down from the platform, his first meeting with the head of the law firm he joined right after law school and how he'd so completely impressed him and his colleagues, about his initial private interview with Crampton before declaring against him, the campaign against Crampton and how valiantly the old man had fought him every inch of the way and about the early morning after the results were in when he made love to Sue—their last time together.

He again thought about the curious impulse that makes a man review all he is as he finds himself thrust into perilous circumstances that will test his body and soul so thoroughly. Although he'd been there not long before, he felt a long, way from the little town of Moran where he grew up.

David Murchison, his administrative assistant, was thirty-two years old, a former law student with him at the University of Wyoming and recently his partner in their own firm. He was always looking for the light side of life, seldom burdened with heavy thoughts. He used Dave as a release valve. When Matt asked him about taking the job, he said, "Sure, Matt, why not? I might as well be second banana in Washington as Cheyenne."

Liz Woodbury was a middle-aged secretary he hired when he first joined the firm in Cheyenne. Matt liked her around because she reminded him somewhat of his mother, and he felt guilty for not visiting his parents more than he did. Liz Woodbury was slim and attractive for a fifty-three year old woman and went to certain pains to see that she was. It didn't matter to her what Matt Hawkins planned for her on Wednesdays at half past five. She was going to her hairdresser no matter what court case needed work.

At Dulles, they took a taxi into town to the Washington Hilton on Connecticut Avenue, which Liz chose because it had a good heated pool and she knew Matt liked to swim whenever he had a chance. The management, accustomed to much better than a mere representative from Wyoming, promptly installed him in suite 14K, with a living room, four bedrooms and a kitchen, where they would all live for the next two months.

During the thirty-minute drive from Dulles, Murchison went over various details they would have to see to. Matt had to call on the current speaker, Lamar Perryman, and also on Niles Overton, who was to be the speaker for the next Congress as far as Murchison or anyone else generally knew. Murchison would find out their office suite assignment and would be calling back to Wyoming to arrange for the rest of Hawkins's staff to come down, for files to be shipped, etc.

That night Hawkins went over to see Bill Crampton at his apartment in the old Watergate complex.

In the car, the driver said to him over his shoulder, "New in town?"

Matt frowned. *Was it that obvious?*

"Yes, but I know my way around."

Matt hadn't learned that big-city car service drivers didn't know how to be insulted. Except when it came to a tip.

"Ain't we got a stupid gov'ment, buddy?"

"Oh, I don't know. How do you mean?" He was curious.

"All this shit about that College and the House and the votin' they gotta do. You think they could cut some of the shit and reduce taxes first, wouldn't ya?"

"They might get around to it someday," Matt offered.

"And my God damn dick should drop off from bein' overworked," grunted the driver.

The car moved through the rain down Connecticut Avenue until it reached Pennsylvania Avenue and the White House. The driver didn't speak as they drove past the Executive Mansion and Matt looked at the white edifice, every inch of it shining, even in the downpour, under heavy stark lights.

He felt a shiver move down his spine quickly and the cold November air creep under his skin. He asked the driver to turn up the heat.

In Crampton's apartment Matt took off his raincoat and sat down. Crampton asked if he wanted a drink and he realized that he hadn't had one all day.

"Yes, Bill, Scotch and water." Crampton fixed Matt's drink and himself a Dickel on the rocks and came over to sit by him.

"I used to drink Scotch, too, but for the past ten years all I can stand is bourbon. I can thank Lamar Perryman for that."

"How well do you know the speaker, Bill?" Matt noticed that Crampton looked very tired.

"Well enough. We've both been in the House so long and suffer from the benign neglect of the leadership that we've developed things in common. One of them is bourbon. I like Lamar, though, but he's not easy to know, if you want the truth. A quiet-living, reflective, private man," said Crampton.

"You look as tired as I feel," said Matt, smiling and running a hand through his wavy hair.

"Why not?" laughed Crampton with a heavy groan. "I don't think there's a single politician in this country who's had a minute's sleep in the past forty-eight hours," he added with a laugh. Matt thought again of his good night's sleep and the sex with Sue after the results were in. When he had no clue what was going on.

"Let's talk about the House," said Matt.

Crampton grew serious.

"Well, actually, there's not much we *can* talk about till we caucus." Matt nodded. "It's one thing to tally up the votes strictly along party lines. But in the caucus we'll see how people plan to vote when they declare."

"How do you think it'll boil down as far as I'm concerned?"

Crampton raised his eyebrows for a moment and pursed his lips, sighing deeply.

"Well, again, you can't say till we caucus. By then you'll have a pretty good idea."

Matt smiled weakly. He'd been fingering the tassels on a needlepoint pillow beside him on the sofa. Crampton thought Matt Hawkins suddenly looked much younger than twenty-nine.

"My mother needlepoints," Matt said.

"My wife did that," said Crampton, getting up and returning to the bar by the fireplace to refill his glass.

Matt noticed he hadn't even touched his Scotch and water and quickly gulped it down, the hard liquor burning pleasantly in his throat.

"I'll take another one too, Bill. I need it." He got up and went over to the bar to stand beside Crampton. Matt mixed his own drink.

"You know, Matt, a guy can find out what kind of man he is in a place like Washington." He turned around and leaned against the mantelpiece beside the bar. "That may sound like a bunch of schoolboy malarkey, but," he said, taking a sip of his bourbon and smacking his lips together, "it's a fact. Yes sir, a mighty solid fact."

"Well, I won't let them push me into anything," said Matt, turning to look at Crampton.

"Let's not worry about what they can do to you until we find out how important you'll be," said Crampton smiling reassuringly. "They do have ways, though," he added, his smile gone, "of pulling a man across. They have ways you can't begin to imagine, and just like every man alive, they're all a little different."

Chapter 44
No Luggage

Derek Gilbertson didn't want to valet his car at the Hotel Victor on Ocean Drive because he didn't want to be seen standing in front of the place as he waited for them to bring it back later, so he walked the two blocks around the corner on Collins Avenue where he'd found a parking space and sent a text. The answer came back: "Rm 505."

He jogged up a few steps and entered the beautifully restored Art Deco lobby with its intricately designed terrazzo floor, went to the elevator and took it up a floor to the Vue Terrace Bar overlooking the pool deck. He had a Corona. When he finished, he went back to the elevator and took it to the fifth floor.

He didn't even notice the slightly overweight tourist wearing the faded Hawaiian shirt at the end of the bar drinking a Bud Lite. He mixed in so well with the tourists gathered around him that he virtually disappeared.

As soon as Gilbertson made for the elevator, Sean Walsh followed him and noted that the elevator stopped on the fifth floor. He took the stairs up and saw there was a little seating area at the end of the hallway. He moved a potted palm shrub that partially obscured his seat. Settling down with a magazine, he texted his partner, Wilfredo Zequiera, and told him to take up a position outside the hotel across the street and wait for Gilbertson to come out. Fredo would pick up the tail on Gilbertson and Walsh would follow the person Gilbertson was meeting in Room 505.

It took only fifty-five minutes for them to finish their business. Gilbertson, slipping on his suit jacket, came out adjusting his necktie and went for the stairs. Six minutes later, a dark-haired woman came out after him. She took the elevator.

Walsh knew he wouldn't have to do any background checks to find out her identity, because he already knew who she was. She was Wilma Kassman, the tough-as-nails manager of the hottest nightclub in South Beach, the Kremlin. Walsh's eyebrows went up in admiration. He hadn't known Derek Gilbertson had it in him to be fucking one of the hottest chicks in town as well as one of the most powerful people in the South Beach nightlife industry.

But Walsh knew Gilbertson hadn't been in there for fifty-five minutes with Wilma playing Tiddlywinks.

He texted Fredo to let Gilbertson go and to meet him at the Vue Terrace Bar. They were done for the day.

Their boss Jack Houston St. Clair was going to buy them two well-deserved high-priced beers, and there was nothing he could do to stop it because he was in Washington.

Chapter 45
The Thomas Jefferson Suite

"Well, this is grand," said Governor St. Clair as he walked hand-in-hand with Sofia into their suite at the Willard, followed by a bevy of staffers.

"You couldn't get a better location. We're at 1401 Pennsylvania Avenue," said Jack.

"You can walk to the White House," said Sofia.

"Let's hope we don't have to crawl," said St. Clair.

"And here, when you pick up the phone, you don't get the world on the other end," said Jack.

"No," said the Governor, "you get room service."

Everybody laughed.

The staff spread out in the living and dining rooms and bellmen took Jack's things to one of the rooms they'd added onto the suite. St. Clair's body man took charge of getting his clothes arranged and Sofia's assistant did the same thing.

Dunc Olcott and others came pouring in with a hundred things to go over.

"Thurston's making more noise at eleven," said Olcott.

"God, will the man never shut up," said St. Clair.

Over their shoulder, one of the staffers spoke into a cell phone.

"Yes, he's in the Thomas Jefferson Suite."

Olcott turned to St. Clair.

"Maybe after you've left the Presidency, they'll name a suite like this after you."

"I just hope I do better than a landfill," said St. Clair with a sardonic smile. "Turn on the TV and let's see what Thurston has to say."

* * *

While St. Clair had been relatively discreet with his public statements about the Russian invasion, Thurston had been burning up the airwaves, appearing on every news program that would have him: Fox, NBC, ABC, CBS, CNN, all of them—*Good Morning America*, the *Today Show*, everything. Just blasting away at the Russians. He blamed Norwalk for "encouraging" the Russians in their "reckless military adventures."

In the middle of Thurston's latest diatribe, all the networks cut him off when Norwalk appeared in the White House Press Room to denounce Thurston's hotheaded comments, saying they did not befit a potential President-elect who ought to examine his facts before shooting off his mouth.

"You all know I like to do a little reading before I retire, and last night I was cozying up to my latest thriller. And I'd like to point out that when I was reading *Congressional Record*, I took special note that Senator Thurston is *Senator* Thurston." There was laughter throughout the Press Room, which went silent the moment Norwalk's expression changed from playful to dead serious. "This man, this *senator*, is not even the President-elect. He has *not* won this election. Maybe he needs an elementary civics lesson. He does *not* represent the United States government." Norwalk jabbed himself in the chest three times. *"I do."*

The response was electric. Everybody—even Thurston's supporters, seemed to respect Norwalk for bringing Thurston down a notch. He was clearly getting too big for his britches.

St. Clair huddled with his advisors. He'd already issued a statement deploring the Russian advance. Now he issued another statement that said: *Calm heads, we need calm heads.*

Somebody came in and gave Dunc Olcott a sheath of papers marked *URGENT.*

"This is it, Governor," he said, passing it over to St. Clair.

"So this is the Who Stands Where List, eh?"

"That's right."

"All right. Let's study it and then we'll have a senior staff meeting tomorrow morning."

St. Clair got Jack to clear everybody out of the suite, saying that he and Sofia needed a little quiet time to recover from the trip. Sofia actually did go into the beautifully appointed bedroom to lie down.

"Let's make that call," said St. Clair.

Jack picked up the phone.

"Get me the White House."

Jack handed the phone to his dad and poured them drinks from the bar against the wall. They put him through immediately and Jack could hear Norwalk's mellifluous voice in the background. The Governor didn't say much, mostly listened. He said "Yes, Mr.

President" three or four times, but not much more. After he hung up, he turned to Jack and shrugged.

"He said not to worry too much about the Russian advance. That he knew all about it before it happened. Also to email this list over right away to Phil Slanetti. It'll be in your email inbox from Dunc."

"Slanetti. He's still Congressional Liaison, right?"

"Yeah. Slanetti or someone will contact us and we'll go from there. He said he was very optimistic about our chances in the House."

"Where the hell does he get this confidence?" asked Jack, taking the list from his dad.

"I'll be damned if I know. I don't see it at all."

"Neither do I."

"Jack, you're in the detective business."

"Well, a little."

"You see any positive direction in any of this crap?"

Now it was Jack's turn to shrug.

"No. I don't get it. Don't get it at all."

A knock at the door.

"Come in," said Sam.

Three or four staffers came in with other business for his dad. Jack held up the list.

"I'll take care of this, Dad,"

"Right."

Jack's iPhone buzzed in his pocket. He pulled it out and saw the call was from Ramona Fuentes. He went out into the hallway where people were rushing up and down as they worked to turn several rooms into makeshift offices.

"Ramona. Hey, how are you?"

"Fine, Jack, fine. Look, I know how swamped you are with the move to Washington and the suddenness of everything, but I'm curious to know—have you found out anything about Derek?"

"Ramona, let me check in with the office and I'll get back to you in five."

"Thanks for taking the time, Jack."

"No problem."

He hung up and walked down a couple of doors where some campaign operatives were setting up an office. He slipped into one that looked less hectic than the others and ran into a pretty blonde campaign staffer.

"Sorry. I just need a quiet corner to make a call."

"I have a quiet corner," she said. "In fact, four of them, including one with a window."

"Thanks," he smiled at her as he moved to the corner with the window overlooking Pennsylvania Avenue. He thought back to his tempestuous time with Raven and knew that if she'd seen him so much as smile at this cute little blonde that she'd rip his balls off and grind them up to put in that Cuban dish they called *picadillo.* He rolled his eyes and shook his head in disbelief that he could have been with Raven for so long. *That woman*, he thought.

He went to his email, found The List, and emailed it to Phil Slanetti. Then he called his office.

"The St. Clair Agency," came Adele Teran's voice on the other end.

"Hey, Adele. It's Jack."

"Yes, sir?"

"Who's around?"

"Sean's in the office, Fredo's in the field."

Sean Walsh came on the line.

"Yeah, boss?"

"What's the latest on the Gilbertson surveillance?"

Walsh told him that they'd tailed him to a meeting with a man, as yet unidentified, at Enriquetta's, and that later he visited Wilma Kassman at the Victor for what had to be, in Walsh's humble opinion, sex.

"Wow," Jack said in a low voice. "Wilma Kassman. That's saying something."

"It sure is," Walsh agreed.

"You sure it was sex?"

"He was pulling on his jacket, patting down his hair and tightening his tie when he came out the door, Jack."

"That looks like sex to me."

"Yeah. I left out the part with his shit-eatin' grin."

"You're a poet with words, Sean."

"That's me."

"The guy Derek met with at Enriquetta's—"

"His plate's registered to a company in Delaware. That's why he's been hard to ID. But I got some pretty good pics."

"OK. Keep on it. We need to know who that guy was."

"It's something, because they didn't even go into Enriquetta's, or hang out at the window where you get the coffee, you know? They stood outside under a clump of palm trees talking for about ten minutes."

"No one to overhear them."

"That's right."

"OK. I'll be back in a couple of days for an overnight, then back up here to help Dad."

"OK, boss. See you then."

"Yeah. And when you go out again on Gilbertson, take Fredo and the van. Get some audio."

"You got it, boss."

He hung up, thought a minute, much more about the guy under the palm trees than about Wilma Kassman (although that was something to think about as well—what could be behind *that* connection?), and then called Ramona back to fill her in.

"I think we're more interested in the man he met at Enriquetta's than we are Wilma Kassman."

"No question," Ramona agreed. "Stay on him. There's something, oh—not quite right about him. I just don't know what."

"We'll find out, Ramona."

"I'm sure you will, Jack. Best to Sam and Sofia."

"You bet."

Jack turned back to the pretty blonde staffer.

"Thank you," he smiled. "What's your name?"

"Shelly. Shelly Crenshaw."

"Well, thank you again, Shelly Crenshaw. Where are you from?"

"Birmingham."

"Birmingham. I love Birmingham. Used to play golf at the Mountain Brook Club."

"It's still there," said Shelly, impressed. "Pretty ritzy, the Mountain Brook Club."

"Yes, it is. I'm sort of in the golf course business, so I've played a lot of them."

"I've seen pictures of the course on St. Clair Island."

"Not nearly as challenging as the Mountain Brook course."

"It's all those hills."

"Steep hills, as I recall."

She laughed. There was a slight pause that in another time of his life he would have filled with an offer to meet her later in the lobby bar for a drink, but since he was seeing Babe, he exiled the very idea of such a thought from his overworked mind.

"Well, thanks again," he said instead.

She nodded.

"Anytime."

Jack nodded back, bit his lower lip and went back out into the hallway.

Chapter 46
The Big Leagues

Matt and Liz watched the Security Council proceedings on TV from the Hilton. Dave was over in the New House Office Building seeing to their suite. The current Congress convened that morning and for that reason he didn't try to call either Perryman or Overton, knowing they'd be busy and have no time for him.

Matt watched the Russian ambassador to the United Nations as he gently pulled his earphone out and sipped delicately from a glass of water. He smiled and shook his head slowly at the man's calm actions. Liz was furious at his impertinence.

"Those Russians!" she said.

He got a call from Brian Gilbert of Thurston's staff. Gilbert asked him if his public statements supporting Thurston's China policy still stood and if he still supported the candidate.

"Yes, of course I do." he said.

"The senator asked me to thank you, Matt, and he'll be seeing you soon."

"I'm looking forward to meeting him, Brian."

"Well, he's looking forward to meeting you, too," said Gilbert, and Matt could tell he wanted to get off the phone and on to his next call.

"As you know, Matt, the senator is making a speech to the National Press Club this afternoon. We have a table and might be able to squeeze you in if you're free."

That afternoon, he and Murchison went to the National Press Club building where they sought out Brian Gilbert. When they found him, Gilbert greeted them as though he hadn't expected Hawkins to show up. He could get Hawkins in, but because they were so tight for space, Murchison would have to wait outside. Matt met a few congressmen at the table he was shown to, but most representatives were not freshman and were busy with a million other things, mainly trying to persuade others in their delegations to switch sides.

There was no such arguing in the Wyoming delegation, because all of it sat with Matt Hawkins in the National Press Club.

He met Mayor Edward Healy and two other freshmen, Sam Carberry and Calvin Brown, who followed Healy around like two underpaid aides. He met a Democratic congressman from Arizona who told him he should be with Republican Ernest Rylsky trying to bring him over. Rylsky was one of four Republican congressmen from Arizona. But he was leaning with the four Democrats because he was staunchly for Thurston's China policy but *not* for Thurston. He was meeting right then with Governor St. Clair and this made the Democratic congressman from Arizona furious because he knew that if Rylsky didn't switch, the state's vote wouldn't be worth anything to St. Clair.

Hawkins also met Wade Trexler of Rhode Island, one of two Democrats from that state constituting the state delegation. Trexler told him, when he found out Matt supported Thurston, that he'd just met with his colleague from Rhode Island, who was strongly for St. Clair. If the other man voted for St. Clair, Trexler's vote wouldn't be any good to Thurston, either. Matt knew Trexler well from his reputation. He was a violently opinionated man and viciously hated St. Clair. He told Matt over and over again that he would somehow convince his Democratic colleague not to vote for St. Clair. Matt didn't doubt he could do it.

Matt listened carefully to Thurston's speech, full of passion and bombastic rhetoric against Russia, Norwalk and St. Clair. Afterward, he met Thurston briefly, Brian Gilbert whispering in his ear who Matt was, Thurston smiling as though Gilbert wasn't even there. He patted Matt on the back and told him he appreciated his support and would remember it when he was in office.

Outside was nuts: a crowded, hectic, screaming scene full of reporters yelling and screaming, trying to get near Thurston as he was led to his car by staff and his Secret Service detail. Matt's mind was full of the excitement, pushing, shoving, the flashing cameras and outstretched arms and microphones all around the candidate.

He happened to walk out of the room with Thurston (part of a gaggle of other people), and quite by accident, after reporters asked Thurston some questions, they turned to him.

"Congressman-elect Hawkins, isn't it?" asked one reporter.

"Yes?"

"What's your feeling about the Russian advance into China?"

"I'm furious that they'd take such a bold unilateral step," he began, trying to answer with the same forcefulness and directness he used back in Wyoming. He saw Thurston lean in towards an aide who whispered something in his ear. He let Matt go on for a few seconds before patting him on the shoulder and interrupting.

"The new representative from Wyoming completely supports my position."

"This is true," Hawkins said. "I do."

"That'll be all for now, everybody," said Thurston as he moved away.

As he left, he took the crowd with him, and Matt found himself alone with Murchison.

"Well, we're in the big leagues now, Matt."

"Yeah. The big leagues."

Chapter 47
Special Session

William R. Crampton—that is, *Congressman* William R. Crampton, at least for another couple of months—sat in his customary seat in the House chamber and looked at the carved woodwork behind the speaker's chair in a way he'd never seen it before. He found himself noticing things he'd *never* noticed in his God knows how many years of service to the Cowboy State. He surmised it was because he knew he'd never get to look at all of it from the same perspective after Matt Hawkins took his place in the new Congress.

But here he was, a member of the lame-duck Congress called back to Washington by President Norwalk to pass a resolution supporting the fifty state legislatures in their emergency effort to pass laws enforcing electors to vote according to the "slates" they represented.

It was largely a symbolic measure. The Constitution relegated to the *states*, not the federal government, the right to set their own electoral rules when it came to Presidential elections.

The members were milling about chatting with one another before the House was called to order. Crampton watched as Lamar Perryman came down from the speaker's chair to go over a procedural matter with the clerk.

In a few minutes Perryman was working his way up the aisle and stopped by Crampton's seat.

"I'm sorry to hear you won't be with us next session, Bill," Perryman said in his drawl, sweet as molasses, resting a wrinkled hand on his shoulder.

"We all gotta go sometime, Lamar."

"I don't know what I'd do if they tossed me out."

"I feel the same way, Lamar."

"You put up a pretty good fight going independent."

"Not good enough to beat that Hawkins fella."

"What kinda boy *is* he, Bill?"

Perryman was mindful that Wyoming was one of the few states that had a single congressman, a fact that could—*might*—make this Hawkins fellow important in the coming vote.

"Oh, he's a nice boy, Lamar. You'll like him. Never been out of the state of Wyoming before. Take him under your wing, will you?"

"I most certainly will take care of him, Bill. Are you staying in Washington or going back home after the special session."

"I'm thinking of staying, Lamar. I'm thinking I'd go crazy back home, day in, day out."

"Might drum up some lobbying work," Perryman suggested. "Worst thing in the world is havin' nothin' to do, nothin' to get up for. *Stay here, old friend.*"

They set a date for dinner and parted ways when the sergeant at arms came to get Perryman to begin the session.

Chapter 48
The Raging War

Meanwhile, an emergency session of the U.N. Security Council was currently under way in New York, called by China to denounce the Russian invasion.

Norwalk had been on the phone to the U.S. ambassador with strict instructions to *stay out* of the screaming match bound to ignite between the Chinese and Russian ambassadors.

And that's what he did when his turn came to speak. He deplored the invasion (without condemning it), appealed to all parties for calm (they were practically throwing their translation earpieces at each other), begged the Chinese to discontinue their provocative water policy (they adamantly refused), insisted (mildly) the Russians pull back across the borders (they refused).

The Russian and Chinese ambassadors resumed their cacophonous raging, each louder than the other, the Russian baritone sounding comically at odds with the high-pitched squeak of the Chinaman's prattle.

The ambassador glanced at his watch just as the secretary general called for a two hour break.

Perfect. The ambassador smiled. He wouldn't have to forego his lunch meeting at Thomas Keller's famed restaurant, Per Se, where an assistant was even now holding his place with a beautiful Puerto Rican hooker ("party of three?") arranged by a close friend in the French legation. His limo was waiting outside. An hour at Per Se, and hour at his assistant's apartment with the hot Puerto Rican hooker—he'd be back just in time for the afternoon session.

* * *

On the other side of the world, the war raged in the Xinjiang desert on China's western frontier, and in Mongolia to the north.

After a strong initial assault, the main Russian advance force was cut off when hundreds of thousands of Chinese forces emerged from the hidden tunnels in the mountainous area of the Xinjiang's southwestern region. The Chinese effectively trapped the Russians in the worst part of the desert, and cut off their supply lines.

The Chinese Air Force battled valiantly the first two days, which kept the Russian land forces under great pressure, but superior Russian air power was starting to take its toll. Their fighter pilots were vastly more experienced than the Chinese. And the Chinese were outnumbered.

At night, most of the Chinese troops retreated to the relative comfort of their tunnels while the Russians had to maintain their position in the freezing nighttime desert. When a sandstorm rose up the second night, the Chinese for the most part were underground, and the Russians suffered mightily against the sand crystals whipping away at them at forty miles per hour.

The next morning half the Chinese forces drove the Russians even deeper into the desert while the other half staved off a fierce assault from the Russian rear guard sent in to rescue the army trapped in the desert.

Things were tilting in favor of the Russians in the north, however. When his forces threatened the Mongolian capital of Ulaanbaatar, Field Marshal Tulevgin hopped on a jet to personally oversee the operation. He caught some heat from his superiors in Moscow, but after only one day in the north supervising operations, his troops had surrounded Ulaanbaatar and forced it to surrender. This was enough to shut up the naysayers in Moscow.

The Chinese had been forced to bring in over a half million reinforcements to prevent the Russians from pouring south from Mongolia into China proper.

That was fine with Tulevgin, so he took the opportunity of this break in the action on the northern front to return immediately to the Xinjiang, hoping to convince Moscow to let him bring in additional reinforcements to relieve the units trapped in the desert, which he was forced now to supply by air.

As Tulevgin's plane circled for a landing at a military airport outside Panfilov, he was looking out the window and still fuming about the fools up the chain of command in Moscow. They wouldn't let him move a full *half* of his troops up and throw them into the fight. They didn't want the international community to think they were being "too aggressive."

"Too aggressive!" he snapped to no one in particular.

"Excuse me, sir?" asked an aide.

"What? Oh, nothing. Nothing."

He looked back out the window and wondered how generals were expected to win wars if they were afraid of being "too aggressive."

* * *

As Marshal Tulevgin's plane made its approach to the runway outside Panfilov, General Yin was begging his superiors in Beijing to maintain a "conservative defensive position." Many of the Chinese leaders wanted Yin to crush the Russians they had outmaneuvered in the Xinjiang.

General Yin argued—it was a delicate argument since he was not a politician and these men in Beijing were the first to remind him of it—that the Chinese should "contain" the Russians until the international community brought enough pressure on the Russians to withdraw. Then the Chinese would look like beneficent winners by opening their ranks to let the Russians return to their border—without the slaughter that would occur if Yin moved all his forces against them.

Chapter 49
Pressure Points

The next day, Ambassador Kornilevski was called to a meeting at the White House, and when he was shown into the Oval Office, he found the President sitting there not only with Secretary of State Uptigrow, but also the Joint Chiefs of Staff. Eric Stathis stood in the corner.

"Welcome, Mr. Ambassador," Norwalk said as he rose from the sofa and shook the Russian's hand. He was served a cup of coffee and Norwalk got right to the point.

"We want assurances that Russia is not invading China to assert some old territorial claims you've had in the north."

"But we have given you every assurrance, Mr. President, and . . ."

"We need something more so I can sell this to the American people."

Kornilevski looked at the military men festooned with ribbons and medals.

"What did you have in mind?"

"We want you to halt your invasion at the captial of Ulaanbaatar, long enough for us to see if we can work on a ceasefire proposal at the U.N."

Kornilevski took a look at the grim faces on the sofa across from him. A warm fire crackled in the fireplace. He glanced over Norwalk's shoulder through the windows overlooking the South Lawn. Though it had stopped earlier, snow now drifted down.

"I'll contact Moscow and get back to you this afternoon, Mr. President."

Norwalk stood and shook the Russian's hand. Appointments Secretary Roebuck escorted Kornilevski from the room.

Norwalk glanced around to the others, let out a sigh of relief and sat back down in his chair by the fireplace.

"One of those meetings you have to have, just for the record, you know?"

Everybody murmured agreement as Eric Stathis moved forward, took a chair and nodded to Army Chief of Staff General Flanagan, who opened a slim folder.

"I have the status report on Operation Dim Sum, Mr. President."

Stathis smiled.

"They've made significant progress, Mr. President."

"We've had several teams around the world working on this since you told us what Lebedyev came to see you about."

"I know it's pretty short notice to take out their computer systems, General," said Norwalk.

"Looks like one of the cyber teams at our base in Ramstein has broken through their firewalls."

"Yeah?"

"They should know in a couple of hours if the virus they planted will work."

"If it will work? And what about *when* it will work?"

"Yes, Mr. President, and when it will work."

Norwalk leaned back in his chair and rubbed his chin with his thumb and index finger.

"General, have our own people ever worked up a fake cyber attack on our national electrical grid?"

"Sir?"

"If we can take down systems using computer hackers—the way we're trying to do now in China and the way we did with the Iranian nuclear program—seems to me like these same weapons will be used against us someday."

"It's always possible, Mr. President."

Norwalk nodded.

"And those drones we use over there—forgive me, General—with such a devil-may-care attitude, killing civilians and then pretending we didn't. What's going to happen when these terrorists get hold of them and start using them in New York or Charleston or wherever the hell they want?"

"We have to keep the technology out of their hands, Mr. President," said Flanagan.

Norwalk snorted.

"Said with a straight face, General. Yeah, we've done a really professional job protecting our technology," said Norwalk, doing nothing to disguise a hard edge of sarcasm. "The Chinese, the Russians—they're all master thieves. What a nightmare."

Everybody just stared at Norwalk until he realized he'd said too much, maybe gone too far. You could never be sure if these military types might not turn on you with no advance warning.

"That's all. Keep me advised—I want hour-by-hour updates—on all this cyber crap—you understand, General?"

"Yes, Mr. President."

* * *

In Beijing two hours later, the defense minister brought the country's chief engineer along with his team to an urgent meeting with Chinese President Wu Qinglin.

A massive central computer malfunction had shut down the software that controled the water release systems and network of locks along the Mao Canal, derailing the timetable to open the massive project.

What?" screamed Qinglin. "My entire foreign policy is based on the timetable *you* gave me!" he thundered, the threat of death in his eye.

The engineer tried to explain the details, but Qinglin cut him off.

"I don't care about all that," he yelled. "How long? *How long?"*

"A week. A month. *We can't be sure!"*

"Get out!" Qinglin ordered. As soon as they were out, he called an emergency meeting of his closest advisors.

An hour later China issued a communiqué announcing that Beijing had completed construction of the Mao Canal and was ready to activate it. But before diverting the waters of the Black Irtysh into it, China threatened to release the waters in the reservoir, immediately flooding hundreds of thousands of acres of Russian land unless the Russians halted their advance immediately.

It was the biggest bluff Qinglin had ever made in his life.

But it was enough to get the world's attention.

The Kremlin sent out orders within the hour to all Russian units to stop in their tracks and prepare defensive positions.

The armed forces of the United States, Great Britain, France, Germany, Japan, India, Canada and twenty-three other countries went on high alert.

* * *

In New York, at the very moment the communiqué was issued, the Security Council was meeting after a longer-than-normal two-hour lunch break.

In the heat of accusatory speeches coming from the Russian and Chinese ambassadors, the French ambassador spontaneously proposed an immediate ceasefire—without consulting his government.

There was a sudden silence at the famous big round table, a rare enough occurrence on its own. Suddenly, all the ambassadors agreed to it, also without consulting their governments, and, to the shock of everyone in the diplomatic community everywhere in the world, an uneasy ceasefire took effect immediately.

A NOTE FROM THE AUTHOR

GET THE NEXT BOOK IN THIS SERIES – FREE

Building a relationship with my readers is the very best thing about writing.

I occasionally send newsletters with details on new releases, special offers and other bits of news relating to Jack Houston St. Clair and the world he lives in, as well as books I'm reading that I think might interest you.

As an encouragement to sign up for my mailing list, I'll send you the second book in the St. Clair series **ABSOLUTELY FREE,** with no strings attached.

To get the Ebook for free, just send me an email so I will know where to end the download link. Click here so that I know where to send it:

<u>ridge@ridgeking.com</u>

Enjoy this book? You can make a big difference.

Reviews are the most powerful tools in my arsenal when it comes to getting attention for my books. Much as I'd like to, I don't have a financial muscle of a New York publisher. I can't take out full-page ads in the newspaper or put posters on the subway.

(Not yet, anyway.)

But I do have something much more powerful and effective than that, and it's something that those publishers would kill to get their hands on.

A committed and loyal bunch of readers.

Honest reviews of my books help bring them to the attention of other readers.

If you've enjoyed this book, I would very much appreciate if you could spend just a couple of minutes leaving a review (it can be as short as you like).

Thank you very much.

One more thing. I love to hear from readers. And I answer each email personally. So if the urge moves you, please feel free to drop me a line.

ridge@ridgeking.com

CPSIA information can be obtained
at www.ICGtesting.com
Printed in the USA
BVHW061355040321
601715BV00007B/465